W9-BOK-479

WHEN
DAD
KILLED
MOM

WHEN
DAD
KILLED
MOM

JULIUS LESTER

Silver Whistle
Harcourt, Inc.
San Diego   New York   London

www.harcourt.com

Silver Whistle is a trademark of Harcourt, Inc., registered in
the United States of America and/or other jurisdictions.

Library of Congress Cataloging-in-Publication Data
Lester, Julius.
When Dad killed Mom/Julius Lester.
p.   cm.
"Silver Whistle."
Summary: When Jenna and Jeremy's father shoots and kills their artist
mother, they struggle to slowly rebuild a functioning family.
[1. Murder—Fiction.   2. Family problems—Fiction.
3. Artists—Fiction.   4. Brothers and sisters—Fiction.
5. Parent and child—Fiction.]   I. Title.
PZ7.L5629Wj   2001
[Fic]—dc21   00-12033
ISBN 0-15-216305-0

Text set in Minion
Designed by Cathy Riggs

First edition
H G F E D C B A

Printed in the United States of America

For Lián,
my youngest one,

and

Milan,
my only one

AUTUMN

Jeremy

My mother is dead.

Dad killed her.

I was in the art room with my class, working on a drawing of the tree next to the old barn Mom made into her studio, the tree whose branches I look at from the couch where I lie sometimes when she is drawing or painting. Anybody who saw my drawing would think it was only a birch tree. Only I knew it was the one outside the window next to the old barn Mom made into her studio.

When the classroom door opened, I didn't look up. I was concentrating really hard, like Mom does when she sits on the stool at her drawing table. I wanted to finish the drawing so I could show it to her when I got home. She says I remind her of herself when she was twelve—serious and hardworking. She says she likes to see things through my eyes, that I see things as they are and that's what it takes to be an artist.

I didn't hear Miss Albright, the art teacher, come over. I didn't even know she was standing next to me until I felt a hand on my shoulder. It was like I had been asleep or something, because I kind of jumped and looked to see who it was. It's funny how when someone touches you on the shoulder, you almost always look in the direction away from where they touched you. I looked to the left and then realized and looked the other way. I saw pale blue, like the sky at this time of year after the leaves have fallen from the trees but before the first snow. It was Miss Albright's dress. I looked up at her and she seemed worried or concerned about something. I thought she didn't like my drawing and I looked down at it. I can draw almost anything exactly like it is. It's a talent I was born with. I got it from Mom. Not only can she draw anything she sees, she can even draw things she saw a long time ago, like the view of the Golden Gate Bridge from the window of her room at Gran and Grampy's house in San Francisco. I knew there was nothing wrong with my drawing. That tree looked so real you could almost peel off some of the white bark. I was about to ask Miss Albright what she thought was wrong with my drawing when I noticed the principal, Mrs. Worthing, standing behind her. She looked worried, too.

"You need to go with Mrs. Worthing back to your room, Jeremy, and get your coat and books," Miss Albright said, whispering in my ear.

"Why?" I wanted to know. "I want to finish my drawing to show my mom when I get home."

Miss Albright has dark curly hair and her eyes are always laughing. Just looking at her makes me happy. But looking at her this time I felt alone, like when Mom is angry at Dad and I'm afraid they're going to get divorced like all the other kids' parents. Miss Albright was blinking her eyes fast, like I do when I want to cry but don't think I should. That was when I knew something bad had happened.

"Come, Jeremy," Mrs. Worthing said.

4

All the other kids stopped drawing and talking and looked at me as I got up.

"What's the matter?" Evan asked. He's sort of my best friend and was sitting on the other side of the table trying to draw a picture of Jamie Phillips, except Evan can't draw. The only reason I knew it was Jamie Phillips was because I knew he liked her. "You okay?"

I shrugged, but I didn't look at him as I followed Mrs. Worthing out of the room.

"Did something happen to my sister?" I asked as we started down the hall to my room. Jenna is fourteen and goes to the middle school. She's in eighth grade. This past summer she said she was going to the mall to see a movie, but when she came home she had a ring in her navel. Mom was really angry. I had never seen her so angry. Dad thought it was funny and that made Mom even madder. When Jenna said it was Dad's idea that she get it and that he paid for it, Mom slapped him so hard there was a big red splotch on his face. When Mrs. Worthing wouldn't answer me, I figured Jenna must have done something really bad this time.

When we got to my room, it was empty because everybody was in the art room with Miss Albright. I don't know where Mr. Zweig, my teacher, was. I got my coat and hat from my cubby, and the green canvas backpack Mom made for me, and followed Mrs. Worthing through the halls to her office.

We went through the outer office where the secretaries sit and back to Mrs. Worthing's office. PRINCIPAL is painted on the door. When we walked in, I was surprised to see Jenna. She was sitting on a couch to the left of the door. I was so happy to see her that I started to call her "turd face" or something like that. I don't know why, but I call her names when she makes me angry *and* when she makes me happy. I was grinning because I was so glad to see her, and then I noticed that the black stuff she puts around her eyes was all smudged and messy and there were little black trails going down her face like she had been crying.

"Jen?" I said. My voice came out sounding so small I didn't recognize it as me.

She looked up when she heard my voice. "Oh, God, Jeremy!" she said, and rushed over and gave me a hug so hard I almost fell. Jenna is tall like Dad and has dark hair like Mom, except Mom's is almost as short as mine and Jenna's is long. When she bent over to hug me, her hair fell forward and got on my face, and Jen has boobs now and she was pressing my face into them and I didn't know if I was going to suffocate in her boobs or choke to death from all her hair. Then she started crying. Jen had never done anything like that around me, and I wanted to push her away because I was afraid she was going to get snot in my hair, and that was when she said, "Dad killed Rachel."

Rachel is my mom's name. Jenna started calling her that this summer. Mom hated it and told Jenna to call her Mom, and Jenna mostly would, but sometimes I think Jenna did it just to make Mom mad. This summer it seemed like anything Mom said to Jenna made her angry, and anything Jenna said to Mom made *her* angry. And Mom really gets angry when Dad takes Jenna's side, but he's done that ever since I can remember.

It took me a few seconds to realize Jenna was talking about Mom, that she was saying Mom was dead and that Dad had killed her. I didn't believe her and pushed her away from me.

"Stop it, Jenna! That's not funny!" I yelled. *Wait until Mom hears about this one! Jenna will really be in trouble. Even Dad will probably be mad at her.*

I expected to see the little glint Jenna gets in her eyes when she's being mean, but all I saw was tears.

"Jen?" I said, my voice small again.

"I'm sorry, Jeremy," Mrs. Worthing said softly. She put her arms around both our shoulders and led us over to the couch and sat down between us. I didn't want to hurt her feelings or any-thing, but I didn't want Mrs. Worthing touching me and I moved out from under her arm and scooted to the end of the couch. Jenna didn't move, however, but seemed to nestle in closer to Mrs. Worthing, who put both arms around her.

It's not that I don't like Mrs. Worthing. She's really nice and says good morning to all the kids as they get off the bus. She knows everybody by name, and that's a lot of names! I don't ride the bus, because school is close to our house, especially when I take the shortcut through the cemetery. The only thing wrong with Mrs. Worthing is that she's tall and skinny, like a wish that's not going to make it. To give good hugs you have to have some soft places, and Mrs. Worthing looks hard all over.

Me, Jenna, and Mrs. Worthing have just been sitting here. Nobody knows what to say. I sure don't. Jenna is sobbing and crying and sniffing all at the same time, and I almost burst out laughing when I think about all the snot that's going to get on Mrs. Worthing's dress. Then I feel kind of stupid for wanting to laugh, but I don't know what to feel or think or do. I wish I could cry, like Jenna, but with her you never know how much is real and how much is Jenna just being Jenna. Mom calls her Sarah Bernhardt. She was some great actress from long time ago, and Mom said that when Jenna was born, she didn't cry; she emoted. I'm not sure what that means, but it sounds like Jen.

"What—what happened?" I ask, mainly to try and shut Jenna up with all her crying.

Mrs. Worthing looks at me. Her mouth opens like she's going to say something and then closes again, like she's not sure she should.

"Is Dad in jail?" Jenna asks, her crying quieter now.

"I don't know," Mrs. Worthing says so softly that I can barely hear her.

"Did it happen at home?" I need to know. "I mean, are we

going to go home and there'll be blood all over the floor or something?"

Mrs. Worthing sighs and looks at me again. "Your mother was in town around ten this morning—"

"She went to get the *New York Times* at Sutter's," Jenna and I say at almost the same time, chuckling. Sutter's is a store in the center of town where you can buy birthday cards, stationery stuff, school supplies, newspapers, and magazines. Mother goes there every morning to get the paper, and then to Café DiCarlo down the street, where she sits at the table in the corner by the window and has coffee and a Danish and reads the paper. Everybody in town knows it's Mom's table. She stays up late every night drawing or painting and doesn't get up until nine or so and then goes into town to get the paper and have coffee. When we were little, Dad got us ready for school.

"When she came out, your— Eric shot her."

"Oh, God! Oh, God! Oh, God!" Jenna screams.

I don't believe it. This is all some sick joke everybody's playing on us, and when I get home it'll be like every day. I'll walk in the house, run up to my room and drop my stuff on the bed, then hurry down and Mom'll be sitting at the kitchen table, drinking coffee. She'll give me a big hug, and I'll feel her breasts beneath my cheek and get that nice funny feeling and want to stay pressed against her for a long time because that feeling seems like it wants to take me somewhere, but Mom doesn't let me hug her for a long time anymore, and she'll go to the stove where there'll be a pot of soup cooking or she'll take a loaf of tomato-parmesan bread out of the oven and make me a cup of some kind of herb tea, and I'll show her my drawing. My drawing! I left it in the art room. I have to get it. I have to get it to show Mom!

"Mrs. Worthing, I have to get my drawing, the one I was working on. I want to show it to my mother when I get home."

"Are you thick or what?" Jenna says. "Didn't you hear what

Mrs. Worthing said? Dad killed Rachel. She's dead, Jeremy. She's dead!" Jenna's face looks like a dirty window.

"I have to get my drawing!" I say firmly. "I have to!" And I run out of the office.

Jenna

I still hate Mrs. Worthing from the time I was in fifth grade and Andrea Martin, that bitch, told her I was the one who had drawn the picture of a vagina which had mysteriously appeared on the wall in the girls' bathroom. Mrs. Worthing called Rachel, and I had to stay after school and wash it off. I was really pissed because I had done it in oil crayon, figuring it would be up there a while.

When Mom saw it she was impressed by how realistic my drawing was. I had put in the labia major and the labia minor and all the folds of the vaginal lips like petals of a flower. The only part that wasn't strictly right was that I had the clitoris showing and you can't really see it, but what the hell? I had spent a long time sitting on the floor of my room naked, my legs spread, a mirror between them, looking at my vagina. I filled a three-by-five drawing pad with sketches until I could draw it from memory. I thought it was beautiful and it was mine! I had something that was really beautiful but nobody could see it! That didn't make any sense. I wanted to sketch the vaginas of every girl in my class, but I didn't have the nerve to ask anybody.

Fifth grade was the year my body started changing. I got my period and then, suddenly, I had breasts. I felt kind of weird at first, different, and I walked around with stooped shoulders like Grandfather Eric, hoping nobody would notice, but after a while hiding those babies was hopeless. Mom said I could wear baggy sweaters, but I thought, *Screw that!* Why should I have to hide my tits like they're something to be ashamed of? The only other girl in my class who was hit with a hormone bomb was Becky Nixon. We had known each other since nursery school and she'd been Miss Prim-and-Proper even then, but I didn't have anybody else I could really talk to and since she and I now had something in common, I figured I'd talk to her. Plus I was curious to see if hers looked like mine, so one day I asked her if I could see her breasts and I'd let her see mine but she freaked out and told everybody I was a lesbian. Even if I had been, what made her think she was my type? Bitch!

When I grow up I'm going to hire models and draw their vaginas and have an exhibit in a gallery in Soho or somewhere and it'll be room after room of nothing but vaginas and breasts and nipples—African American, Jewish, Asian, white, even Eskimo if I can find an Eskimo woman to let me draw hers—in watercolor, charcoal, oils, computer graphics—and women will come and they'll be amazed at how beautiful vaginas are and how different they look. They say no two people have the same fingerprints. I bet no two women have vaginas that look alike, either.

Mom liked my technique. I think it was the first time she realized I was talented at something besides clothes and makeup. But she thought I had drawn a vagina on the bathroom wall to get attention. That's what she thinks about everything I do and it pisses me off. Anybody can get attention, like that freak Bonnie Adams, who came to school last week with her hair dyed three shades of blue. So I told Rachel that if I had wanted attention I would've signed my name to my vagina fresco. "I did it because I wanted to *teach* the girls something about themselves. We're women! That means something and the first thing it means is that your vagina belongs to you. It's between *your* legs, right? Then it's yours! But how can women know it's theirs when they can't see it? Men hold and see their penises several times a day. Not only can't you hold a vagina, it's got so many different parts it's hard to figure out what's what. It's so weird being a girl. We have a hole that has no other purpose except to bleed, have a penis stuck in it, or a baby come out."

I'd tried to talk about stuff like this with other girls, but they just giggled and blushed. Mom said once that artists show people what they have not seen and don't want to see. What's more unseen and unloved than a vagina?

When I finished my tirade, I was amazed I'd said all that to my mom and I figured she was going to ground me for the rest of my life for talking to her about stuff like that, but she was cool. She actually gave me a smile, a real smile, not one of those fake smiles parents put on when a kid does something they really despise but they can't come up with a reason why it's bad. Mom smiled like she was proud of me. It was one of those moments when I could tell she really loved me and I loved her, too, and I can't remember if I ever told her. Damn!

What made me think about that? Oh yeah. Mrs. Worthing, who has her arms around me. I let her hold me because it makes her feel useful, because she has no clue what to do or say. I don't know what you have to study to be the principal of a school, but I doubt there're any classes called "What to Do When a Student's Father Kills Her Mother."

I was in English class, slouched down in my usual seat in the back row, bored to death. Maybe *Red Badge of Courage* was a great book once, but not anymore. This is the nineties and who cares if a bunch of guys want to go out and shoot each other? Let 'em! So I was thinking about Larry Sullivan and wondering if I wanted him to take me to the eighth-grade dance next spring. He's real cute. Guys with dark hair and blue eyes make me weak in the knees. So if I wanted him to take me to the dance, I knew I had to start putting the idea in his head now. Guys are clueless about everything except how to kill each other. Anyway, that's where my mind was and I didn't pay any attention when Mr. Carlton, the principal, stuck his head in the door and beckoned for Mr. Whittier to come into the hallway. But when Mr. Whittier came back a few minutes later and said, "Jenna? Mr. Carlton would like to see you," my attention went on full alert. I got up to leave and Mr. Whittier said, "Take your things."

Everybody in the class started hooting. "What'd you do this time, Jenna?" Larry Sullivan shouted, laughing. That was probably his way of telling me he liked me, but I didn't appreciate it, especially since I was wondering myself what I had done. I couldn't think of a thing. Teachers are always on me because "you aren't performing up to your potential," and Mr. Carlton called me in once to discuss what he called my "attitude problem." I can't help it if I think school is a total bore and totally irrelevant to anything having to do with my life. Sure, I know I'm bright and I know if I studied I could get straight As, but I don't care. Tell me what I have to do to get by and that's what I'll do until I get a teacher with brains enough to challenge me.

So when I went out in the hall, I was prepared not to listen to whatever Mr. Carlton was going to say. I knew I hadn't done *anything,* but from the look on his face I was going to get kicked out of school for sure. Well, whatever he thought I did, I hope I enjoyed it.

Then he said, "Something has happened to your mother. Miss Foster is going to take you over to Forest Green School. That's where your brother is?"

"Yes, but, but, what's going on?"

"I—I'm not really sure. The police called and said that something had happened to your mother and we should get you over to Forest Green to be with your brother. Go to your locker and get your coat and whatever else you need. Miss Foster will be waiting for you in the lobby. And hurry, please!"

I try not to do what adults tell me to, at least not right away, but Mr. Carlton was scaring me. Every day when I saw him in the hallways, I wondered if he knew how ridiculous he looked with that toupee on his head. Did he really think it looked like his hair? If he watched MTV he'd know that bald is cool now. But today he didn't look stupid. He looked serious, like he was not to be messed with. I hurried to my locker, which was over near my homeroom, and then rushed back to the lobby to meet Miss Foster.

Miss Foster is the assistant principal. She's African American and her hair is natural and short and covers her head like black dandelion fluff. Her skin is real dark, so she can wear reds and or-anges and greens and purples and they all blend together. God, I'm so white I could puke! I don't care what Mom thinks, but next summer I'm going to dedicate my life to serious tanning and without any stupid tan lines.

I asked Miss Foster what happened. She either didn't know or wouldn't tell me. But I got scared when I asked her if Mom was all right and she wouldn't say anything. God, it really pisses me off when adults know something but won't tell you because they think you're too young or something. When I got here, Mrs. Worthing knew she'd better tell me something or I was going to pitch a fit. But the last thing I expected her to say was that Dad had shot Rachel. Oh, man! That didn't make any sense at all! I mean, I knew they were having problems but—.

What a fucking mess! What happens now? Where are we going to sleep tonight? Should we go home? And who's going to stay with us? And what about school? No way am I going to school tomorrow. I'm never going back to that place and have people stare at me like I'm some freak on *The Jerry Springer Show*: CHILDREN ALONE: ONE PARENT DEAD, ONE IN JAIL. Half of them will be feeling sorry for me, and the other half who think I'm already crazy will now have proof. Who else but a crazy girl's father would kill her mother?

Anyway, I can't go back to school since I'll probably have to take care of Jeremy now. He's sitting at the end of the couch working on a stupid drawing of that tree out back. He said he had to finish it to show to Mother when we got home. Yeah, right!

I guess I'm kind of jealous. I mean, it's not like *I* really believe any of this, either. So what if I've been hysterical and totally ruined my makeup? That doesn't mean any of this is real. I wish I could see Dad. If I could hear him tell me that he shot Mom, then I'd believe it. Maybe. But sitting here next to Mrs. Worthing, part of me is also trying to figure out which bra to wear tomorrow and how many buttons on my blouse to leave undone and exactly when to bend down so Larry Sullivan can have a peek.

The phone on Mrs. Worthing's desk rings and she goes to answer it. She listens for a moment and then, putting her hand over the mouthpiece, looks at me and Jeremy and asks, "Do you children know someone named Karen?"

I jump off the couch and take the phone from Mrs. Worthing. "Karen? Can you come get us?" And I start sobbing harder than I ever have.

Jeremy

Wednesday, Early Morning

I'm going home. Karen lives in town near the college. That's too far from our house for me to walk, but I can catch a bus in town. I leave a note on the kitchen table telling Karen and Jenna that I've gone home. I grab my green backpack Mom made me, sling it over my shoulder, and go out the front door quietly.

I've always gotten up before everybody else, everybody except Dad. He gets up at six. I always wake up around seven. Jenna and Mom are night people. They'd sleep until noon if they could. Since last summer, though, I've been waking up earlier than Dad. He's been working late at the college or at his office in town and not getting up as early.

That was okay with me since I liked being by myself in the morning. I would be very quiet so as not to wake Mom, who was asleep on the second floor of the studio. I'd let myself out and close the door quietly behind me. I'd cross the yard and let myself in the back door of the house, go upstairs, wash up, brush my teeth, and change clothes. Then I'd get cereal or heat up some frozen waffles in the toaster. When I finished eating, I'd lie on the butcher-block couch in front of the fireplace in the family room and watch CNN Headline News, read a magazine or the paper, or just sit and think about life and stuff like that. Sometimes I'd sit on the deck and watch the morning. I wished Mom would wake up early so I could talk to her about the morning colors and learn which ones she saw that I didn't and which ones I saw that she didn't. Dad doesn't see colors.

When Dad used to get up before me, he'd always make breakfast. He would fix oatmeal from scratch, eggs any way I liked them, French toast, pancakes, or whatever. I liked that part, but the part I didn't like was having to talk with him. He's a psychologist and always wanted to know what I was feeling. Most of the time I'm not feeling much of anything. I mean, I feel hungry sometimes and tired sometimes and sleepy. Mostly I feel happy. Or I did before this past summer. But he'd tell me I had other feelings, feelings about him and Jenna and Mom, that maybe I was angry about something or felt hurt about something. I didn't feel much of anything except wishing he'd stop asking me about my feelings.

It's cold but sunny. It hasn't snowed yet, but it hardly ever does before Thanksgiving. As I walk the three blocks to the bus stop, I wonder what I should get Mom for Christmas. Then I remember. I don't know what to do. It's like Mom is dead but she's the only who knows it. My mind doesn't and neither do my feelings.

It's hard being a kid at Christmastime, because you don't have your own money so you can't buy the presents you really want to buy. Whatever I've ever wanted to buy Mom, Dad said it cost too much. Like how could a present for your mother cost too much? I always end up buying her dumb stuff like handkerchiefs or perfume. She's not a handkerchief or perfume kind of Mom, but Dad said that was what she wanted. But I never saw the handkerchiefs or smelled the perfume on her. Sometimes I think I know better than Dad what Mom likes. There's a big book of paintings by a woman named Georgia something, which I know Mom would really like, but it costs almost a hundred dollars.

I'm glad there's no one at the bus stop. There isn't a lot of traffic yet. The bus will stop in front of the bank, where someone just turned the lights on inside. I wonder if that person knows my dad killed my mom. Maybe that person saw him do it, because Sutter's is right down the street from the bank. I wonder if Mom's blood is on the sidewalk. I should go look and if there is, maybe I could scrape it up and somebody could put it back in her and then she would be okay. I know that's stupid, but I can't help thinking it.

It was all on TV last night. They said that Dad shot Mom and then ran away. The police found him at home, sitting on the front step with the gun pointed at his head like he was going to kill himself. I listened but squeezed my eyes shut. Jenna watched and said Dad looked really upset and was crying. The TV said it took the police a couple of hours before they were able to talk Dad into giving them the gun. Jenna said they showed him being handcuffed and put into a police car, and that was when she started crying again and said she wanted to see him. I told her she could if she wanted to but I never wanted to see him again. She said I was a jerk and I said she was a bigger jerk and Karen told us to stop it and we did. I was waiting for the TV to say why Dad did it, but they said no one knew, and then a commercial for a seafood restaurant came on. But before that the TV said my and Jenna's names, something about we were in seclusion at the home of a family friend.

As the cars stop at the light, I keep my head down and hope nobody will recognize me. People who work at the college and people who live here but work in Summerton have to drive through the center of town. I don't want to see anybody. They'll want to know how I'm feeling. I don't want to feel anything. Maybe then it will be like nothing happened and I'll wake up in a few minutes and hear Mom snoring and grinding her teeth.

The bus to South Birchfield comes. That's where we live. South Birchfield is not separate from Birchfield. It's just what that section of town is called. There's a North Birchfield and a East Birchfield. But west of Birchfield is Summerton, which is a big town, almost a city, with a mall where we go to the movies and McDonald's.

Schoolkids ride the buses for free, so the bus driver doesn't pay any attention to me as I get on. There're only three people on the bus. One of them is holding up the paper, reading it, and on the front page is a picture of my dad holding the gun to his head. Over it the headline reads:

COLLEGE SHRINK KILLS WIFE

Tears as hot as summer fill my eyes, and I hurry quickly down the aisle to the last seat and rub my eyes like I'm sleepy, and the tears go back to wherever tears come from.

The bus is already going by the town common when I realize it is passing Sutter's. I close my eyes, tight. The bus stops at the far end of the common, and I close my eyes even tighter. It sounds like the other people who were on the bus get off and then the bus starts again. I keep my eyes shut until I am sure it is way past Sutter's and the college. When I finally open them, I do it a little bit at a time to make sure I won't see anything I don't want to, and I only open them all the way when I see nothing but houses.

The bus is empty and the driver picks up speed. Only in the afternoon and evening would a lot of people be going this way on the South Birchfield bus. When the bus heads back to town, though, it'll fill up.

"Where're you getting off?" the bus driver calls back to me.

Maybe nowhere, I think. Maybe I'll talk to the driver and he'll just keep driving and driving and driving and the bus will never stop, not even for gas.

"Hey, kid!" The driver yells this time.

I get up and stagger to the front as the bus lurches along. "Uh, you can let me off at Simmons Street," I manage to say. That's the street my school is on and the closest stop to our house.

When the bus stops, the driver says, "Going in early today? Well, never hurt to be an early bird and get that worm, huh? Have a nice day."

I cross to the side of the street away from the school, just in case Mrs. Worthing is already looking for kids to say good morning to. I go past the pond where Dad would take us skating in the winter. The sidewalk starts to go up toward Cemetery Hill. On the other side of the hill are woods, and when you come out of the woods, you're in our yard. Well, it's bigger than a yard. It's more like a field.

Ever since I can remember I would go with Mom to the cemetery and do rubbings of the old gravestones. We used to make up stories about the people. Our favorite was a man named Elijah Barnstable who was born in something like 1697 and died in 1794.

"He was alive at the time of the Declaration of Independence!" Mom exclaimed. We wondered if he had been for it or against it. He could have been friends with George Washington or John Adams or Paul Revere.

In the spring Mom and I picked wildflowers and put them on the graves of some of the people who had been dead for a hundred years or more and didn't have anyone to remember them, especially the little children. A lot of children died young then.

I don't want to go through the cemetery this morning, but if I go the long way around some of the neighbors might see me and I don't want them to.

I keep my eyes down and don't look at any of the gravestones as I go along the gravel road that winds through the cemetery. When I see the path through the woods that comes out in the field back of our house, I break into a run and don't stop until I'm out of the woods and see the red side of Mom's studio.

I walk around to the front of the house, and just as if it were any other day, I go out to the street and take the newspaper from the orange tube. I start toward the house and then remember: the mail. I wonder if Dad got it or maybe the police. I always get it when I come home from school, so I go back out to the street and look in the mailbox. The mail is still there. Sometimes there're a ton of catalogs. Mom likes to cut pictures from the catalogs and paste them into her paintings. I like the ones from Victoria's Secret, but I keep them hidden in my room.

I hear a door closing across the street, and out of the corner of my eye I can see Mrs. Allison. She's a really big woman who wears dresses with bright flowers on them, and she talks a lot. Mom said she was nosy and liked to know everybody's business. If I look over there she'll come flying over here and ask me a lot of questions, so I keep my eyes on the mailbox and the catalogs and letters I'm taking out. I tuck them into the folded newspaper, covering up my dad's picture. As I start up the walk to let myself in the front door, I remember the picture of Dad sitting on the top step holding the gun to his head. I stop and then go around to the back. I hear Mrs. Allison calling my name in a voice that's like a dog howling in the middle of the night, but I pretend like I don't hear her, take out my key, and quickly let myself in the back door.

The house is quiet and dark and cold. Standing in the kitchen, I can hear the clock on the mantel above the fireplace in the family room. Does it know that this is a dead house? No one will ever sit on the couch eating popcorn that was just popped over the logs in the fireplace. Upstairs, where my room and Jenna's and Mom and Dad's are, do the beds know that no one will ever lie on them again?

I put the mail and the paper on the round table in the kitchen, where we eat, and go in the family room. I want to tell the fireplace that it is dead, but no, it isn't. Somebody will buy this house one day and they will make fires there. Maybe. But what if no one will ever buy this house? Who would want to buy the house where a man lived who killed his wife? Who would want to live here?

But maybe someone will come from out of town and they won't care. We didn't ask this house to tell us what it knew before we moved in. Maybe another man who lived here killed his wife. Maybe all the men who lived here killed their wives. Maybe this is a house that makes men kill their wives, and if we had asked the house it would have told us and we would have known and then we could've bought another house. There's a sign on our house that says 1887, the year the main part of the house was built. Maybe I should make a new sign to put next to it: "This house makes men kill their wives. If you are married, do not buy this house."

I go back into the kitchen. The sun is shining through the windows as if my mother is not dead. This is my favorite part of the house. The kitchen is long and wide. Mom said that when she was growing up she wanted a big kitchen with enough space for a large round oak table to eat dinner at and a counter to sit at and eat grilled-cheese sandwiches, and windows everywhere and a deck outside with a table where she could sit and drink coffee in the morning. That was before she started going to town to get the paper and drink coffee. Maybe if she hadn't started doing that, she would be alive. Or maybe he would have shot her here.

I open the drawer where Mom keeps the key to her studio and go back outside. It is chilly but not like winter yet. It is that dead time when all the leaves have fallen and the trees are bare and everything is still and we wait for the cold and the snow. Trees die but they come back to life. I wish my mom was a tree.

The barn is like another house. The downstairs is a big open space with shelves of books along one wall. In the back is a bathroom and kitchen space with a small refrigerator that has a stove on top. Mom could have made coffee for herself and drunk it here. She could have read the paper on the World Wide Web. I would have printed out every article in the paper for her. I'm never going to drink coffee or read the *New York Times*.

I go to the back of the studio where the thermostat is and turn it up. Mom turned it down when she went out yesterday morning. There are two couches down here with big soft cushions. One is on the side where the bookcases are. On Saturday and Sunday afternoons in the winter I liked to lie on the other couch, the one against the windows, and look up into the birch tree or read or nap while Mom works upstairs. She will have classical music on the radio or the CD player and it is warm and I think—I thought—that is how it would always be.

I go up the steps to the loft. There is another couch here that faces the woods. Mom's drawing board is to one side. Being up here is like being outdoors, because three of the walls are glass. The only one that's not is the one facing the house. There are long flat file cabinets filled with sketches and drawings and a cupboard filled with paints and rags and brushes and jars. Nothing in here feels dead.

I take my folded-up drawing from my back pocket and, finding a pushpin, put it on the corkboard where Mom tacks her drawings when she wants to study them. I don't need to study mine. It's for her to see. I know she is dead. At least I know it a little more than I did yesterday. But just because she's dead, it doesn't mean she can't see my drawing.

"There you go, Mom," I say aloud, and I swear I hear her say that I did a good job, especially in the way I got how the top of the tree bends from the weight of all the ice from the big storm a couple of years ago, and I turn around expecting to see her looking at me with a love as deep as the sky, but no one is there.

"Mom?" I call out hesitantly, call out softly, not believing that she won't answer, not believing that she will never answer, not ever again, and the tears as hot as summer rush back into my eyes and spill down my face as I throw myself onto the soft cushions of the couch by the windows, and for the first time, I cry out loud, in sobs that make my chest hurt, cry until my throat feels raw, like it has been cut with a hundred knives.

Jenna

Wednesday Afternoon
KAREN'S HOUSE

I've known Karen all my life. I never thought about it until now. I mean, how weird. It's like I've been living in a soap opera and didn't even know it. But it always seemed natural that Karen would baby-sit me and Jeremy or that she would take us to the movies at the mall or that we would go over to her house on New Year's Eve and stay the night.

It was never a secret that she and my dad had gone to the same college and gotten married. I never wondered what Mom thought about any of it, because she and Karen seemed like friends. Ever since I can remember, Karen would come over for Thanksgiving dinner and bring a rum cake, and at Christmas, a fruitcake she had let soak in wine for a month. She and Mom gave each other birthday and Christmas presents, and I always thought it was pretty cool that my dad had remarried but he and his new wife were friends with the old one.

I know this house as well as I do my own. It's old and sits back from the street, behind hedges so high no one passing by can see in. Our house is old but this one is older—"1810," the little sign on it reads. It was built by somebody who taught at the college, and I guess only people from the college have ever lived in it. Karen's father taught at the college and she works there now, in public relations. Her parents were killed in a car accident when she was a junior at Barnard. Dad and Karen lived here when they were married.

I have my own key, and Jeremy and I each have our own room. Mine is the same one Karen had when she was a girl. It's on the second floor at the opposite end of the hall from the master bedroom, which used to be Karen's parents' and then Dad and Karen's and is now just Karen's. My room looks out over the backyard and the lilac bushes. Karen's dad tried to grow every kind of lilac there is and I guess he came pretty close. Karen tends them now. At the end of the yard is a small gazebo, and sometimes when I need to think or just want to be alone, I go sit there. If it weren't so cold I'd sit there today.

Instead I've been up here in my room since yesterday afternoon. Karen came and tried to talk to me several times, but I kept my back to her and just stared out the window at the gazebo. God,

I can be such a bitch. I mean, Karen came to get us and I was so glad to see her but she looked a wreck. I'd always thought that Karen, of all people, would keep it together, no matter what. I know I'm not being fair but that's just how it is.

I've always liked Karen because she cares about how she looks. Her long dark brown hair seems to shine of itself, as if she put conditioner on each strand one at a time. She usually wears aviator-style glasses that are tinted gray, which is just so cool. I mean, it's not obvious like rose- or yellow-tinted glasses. And Karen has this way of knowing what to wear without overdressing. Whatever she wears is not only exactly right for the occasion, but it is always the best, whether it's jeans or whatever. The cut is just right, the fabric, the accessories. Karen is tall, almost as tall as Dad and he's over six feet. God, they must have looked really cool together. Dad is so good-looking I wonder why he ever married *anybody*. Karen is tall and thin and *so* sophisticated. She could have been a model.

I've always wondered if she was my *real* mother. It would make sense because I'm more like her than Mom. Rachel and I don't have anything in common. Mom could care less about what's fashionable. Her entire wardrobe consists of jeans and men's shirts. And if that's not bad enough, she almost never wears a bra.

That might have been cool in the sixties but this is the nineties, and unless you are going somewhere really glam and want to show some serious cleavage, put on a bra and keep gravity away as long as you can. A couple of summers ago we were at the Cape and Mom and I were changing to go for a swim and I saw her breasts and they weren't bad for somebody her age. They were small, but gravity hadn't sent them too far toward her feet yet. I told her she should start wearing a bra if she didn't want to end up looking like she was posing for *National Geographic*. She shrugged and said she didn't care. Rachel never cared about anything except her damned painting.

She sure as hell didn't know what to do with me and probably wondered if I was really her child as much as I wondered if she was really my mother. Ever since I can remember, I've liked lipstick and eye makeup and nice clothes. When all the other girls in first grade were going to school in pants and jeans, I insisted on wearing dresses or skirts. One Thanksgiving—I must have been around six—I noticed how good Karen looked. I couldn't put it into words then, but I looked at her and I wanted lip gloss to shine on my lips like it had been born there and eye shadow that could make my eyes appear to smolder. I wanted somebody to teach me how to wear clothes that would make people look at me whether they wanted to or not, and it was just so obvious that Karen knew all that and I looked at her and asked, "Will you take me shopping for clothes?"

Mom laughed, looked at Karen, and said, "Would you? Please?" Even though I was glad Mom didn't seem to be hurt or anything, I also felt like she was giving me away. It was like she didn't want to have anything to do with what was most important to me.

Rachel thought I was superficial because I cared about clothes. Even if I was only going to the mall on a Saturday afternoon with some other kids, I was always dressed to kill. I didn't just throw on a pair of jeans and a shirt. I spent hours trying on different combinations of pants, jeans, skirts, blouses, shirts, and sweaters until I found the right color combination, but then I might decide to wear a pair of earrings that didn't go with the clothes and I would have to start all over again. When I finally came downstairs I knew I looked good, and it would've been nice if every once in a while Rachel had said, "You look nice, dear," but she would just look at me. No expression on her face. Dad's face would light up like he had just found a million dollars, but not Mom. Sometimes I wanted to scream, "Why're you looking at me like you just stepped in a pile of dog shit?"

She didn't understand. There is nothing superficial about clothes. When there's something really important I want to get from Dad, I'll wear pigtails and a yellow blouse and jeans. That's one of my little girl looks. But when there's something I want from Mom, I'll put my hair in a braid, wear a dark green blouse, a pair of slacks, and shoes with a little bit of a heel and no makeup. Mom hates makeup. Dad likes it. I play roles. That's all life is, anyway. You play different roles to get what you want and make people react how you want them to. It's public relations. That's all.

But being a bitch is not a role. I wonder sometimes if bitch is the real me. When Karen walked in Miss Worthing's office, I was shocked at how she looked. She hadn't bothered to refresh her makeup and her hair looked scraggly and she looked, well, just ordinary. I know I shouldn't have expected her to look glam after hearing that her ex-husband had murdered his present wife in broad daylight in the center of town. And because of Dad's position at the college, she had probably been talking on the phone to reporters all day, but I was disappointed that she of all people hadn't been able to keep it together. I mean, if I couldn't believe in Karen, who was left?

So I was really cold to her all yesterday. I'm sure she thought I was upset about what had happened and I guess I am. I mean, I don't know. It still doesn't seem real. And I'm feeling guilty, too. I know that's stupid, but I can't help remembering all the times I wished Karen was my real mother and would fantasize about something happening to Rachel, and then I could go live with Karen and she would be my real mother. And now it's happened.

Karen came in my room this morning before she left for work. She whispered my name. I heard her but pretended I was asleep. It would have been nice if I had at least opened my eyes and said good morning. All she wanted was to see if I was all right and it doesn't matter if she thought I was asleep. I knew I wasn't.

I don't know what happens to me at times like that. I don't

mean to be a bitch. Well, that's not entirely true. Sometimes I do. This past summer we were having one of our usual Sunday brunches. They used to be fun until things started going bad. Dad would cook. I think he's a better cook than Mom, though she makes a mean soup. But Dad would make omelettes filled with jelly or cheese, or pancakes so light you hardly had to chew them. There'd be as much bacon or sausage or ham as you wanted to eat or, sometimes, smoked trout or salmon. We would sit around the big table in the kitchen or out on the deck if it was warm, and eat and talk and laugh and listen to some sixties music, which is Dad's favorite. He was my and Jeremy's age in the sixties, so he was too young to go to Woodstock and it's like a part of him still wishes he had been there. That morning he was playing a Mamas and Papas CD, and I guess I got to thinking about them—the Mamas and the Papas—and how what rotten mamas and papas they had been to their children. So I asked him why he and Karen got divorced, and then something really bitchy made me add, "I think she would have been a great mother." And I put this really sweet smile on my face. Mom knew I was being a total bitch, pushed her chair back from the table, and glared at me.

"Then the next time you need a fucking ride to the mall or claim you need a pager or eighty bucks for a pair of shoes, call Karen!" And she was out the door and on her way to the studio, just like that, Jeremy tagging along behind her. I should ask him, but I think that was the last Sunday brunch we had.

"Mom? I'm sorry," I called after her. "I didn't mean anything," which was a total lie.

"Don't be like that, Rachel," Dad yelled. "And Jeremy, you come back here right now." But neither one acted like they heard him. Not that it mattered. Dad trying to be like some stern disciplinarian was a big joke.

I don't know why I said that to Mom. I knew it was going to piss her off. Sometimes I said or did stuff just because I knew it would get to her. It was like I had this power over her. Maybe I didn't have the power to make her love me, but having the power to piss her off was okay. At least she would notice me.

But there was something else that morning. I was pissed because she had moved into the studio and taken Jeremy with her and pissed because she didn't appreciate Dad. It was obvious to me that they weren't happy and that she didn't understand me or him. I understood Dad better than Rachel ever would.

Dad seemed kind of sad that morning, depressed even. He's usually very happy doing brunch, but that Sunday something was off and Rachel didn't even notice. Or if she did, she didn't care. Making Sunday brunches was one of Dad's ways of saying he loved us, and Rachel was clueless. So I was pissed and wanted to make her go away and I did.

But Dad seemed a little annoyed with me. "Sometimes, Jenna, you need to think before you open that mouth of yours. You may not realize it, but you can hurt people with your words," he said.

I nodded like he had just laid some huge revelation on me. One of the first things a kid learns is that you can hurt people with words. You sure as hell aren't big enough to hurt them any other way. All you have is your mouth and you better learn to use it to hurt somebody before they hurt you. The only problem I had growing up was figuring out how much I could say and get away with. But once I learned that all I had to do was put on a sweet smile and speak in a soft voice like I was as innocent as fucking Bambi, I could cut somebody's fucking heart out with a couple of sentences and never get blamed. I always knew what I was saying, and if Dad didn't know that much about me, it made me wonder what kind of psychologist he was. Or maybe he's a great psychologist except when it comes to his own family. After yesterday I guess that's an understatement.

Anyway, I made all the appropriate apology noises and said I would tell Mom I was sorry, which I never did. Now I wish I had. Shit. It's going to be a long fucking life if I start feeling sorry for all the shit I put her through.

Dad hadn't even looked at me when he gave his little reprimand. It was like he had gone through the motions and done his father thing but his mind was somewhere else. He was kind of staring at the table and turning the saltshaker around and around. I'd never seen him like this.

I had asked my friends, none of whose parents are together, how you know when your parents are going to split up. Charlotte's mom has been divorced twice and her dad is on his third marriage, so if anyone knew what to look for, she did. She said my parents had all the signs, like not talking to each other, and when they did, working real hard to be nice. The big one was whether they were still sleeping in the same bed, which they weren't. Mom said she moved to the studio because she wanted to focus on painting. Yeah, right! I couldn't remember a time when painting wasn't all she cared about.

But it was kind of strange because after she moved to the studio I felt like I saw more of her. It seemed like we made a point to eat dinner together every night and afterward Mom would be around for a couple of hours and the four of us would play cards and just hang out together.

But then, all of a sudden, she would be gone. I never understood. Was it something I said? Did she have a time limit on how long she could stay? One minute she was listening to you like there was nothing else in the world she wanted to do, and the next, she was gone. Sometimes she said good night like a normal person. A lot of times, though, she just got up in the middle of a sentence and walked out the back door, Jeremy tagging along like a homeless puppy.

But I didn't care. All it meant was that I could have Dad to myself. He and I would stay up late, talking, and he talked to me like I wasn't a kid but, well, like I was Mom, or who he wished Mom was.

That Sunday it seemed like my question about him and Karen getting divorced made him remember, because he started talking about her and there was a sadness in his voice, like he missed her. She went to Barnard and he to Columbia. Then her parents got killed and Dad and Karen got married the following year when they graduated. I got the impression that Karen's dad had a lot of money and that Karen paid for Dad to go to graduate school while she got a P.R. job with some publisher. Then just as Dad was finishing up his Ph.D., the job at the college opened up. He went for it, got it, and they moved here.

I had heard parts of the story when Mom, Dad, and Karen would talk, but Dad put it all together that Sunday. What blew me away, though, was him telling me that he and Karen had had a kid and she died. Dad wouldn't go into any details, but I got the feeling something really bad happened, like Karen had accidentally drowned the baby in the bathtub or something. I really wanted to know what it was. If I had pushed him, Dad would've told me. He can't say no to me, which, according to Mom, is part of my problem. But he had a look on his face like it was hurting him to remember so I let it alone. Whatever happened, that seemed to be what destroyed the marriage.

Not too many months after the baby died, Rachel Pierce came to Birchfield College as artist-in-residence, and she and Dad met at the opening of an art show. I've watched enough movies on HBO and Showtime, not to mention soap operas, that I can fill in the blanks. Grieving father estranged from his wife meets attractive, dark-haired artist from San Francisco. I was around nine or ten when I realized my parents' wedding anniversary was just three months before my birthday.

I've always been smart in a worldly kind of way. Probably comes from watching TV all my life. Dad thought it was okay for me to watch Sally Jesse and Jerry Springer when I was little. He said I needed to know how the world really was. Mom said that wasn't how the world was. I wonder what she thinks now.

Dad got real quiet after he told me about the baby that had died and I thought he was done talking. I didn't know what to say. It was weird because sometimes I like it when he talks to me like I'm an adult, but other times I kind of wished he treated me like a kid, because I don't know what I'm supposed to say or do when he lays something heavy on me.

I was just about ready to mumble something about how hard that must have been or some bullshit and get out of there when Dad stood up as if he was going to clear the table and said, "You have to promise that you will never tell Rachel what I'm about to tell you. I don't care how angry you ever get at your mother or how much you might want to hurt her one day, if you ever tell her this you'll destroy my relationship with you."

Dad had never spoken to me like that and I knew I had better take him seriously. "I promise, Dad. I promise."

He nodded. "Rachel knows that Karen and I had a child, of course. But Karen and I agreed that she should never know that our little girl's name was Jenna."

I almost shit! I saw the tears in his eyes and I almost knocked the table over getting around it to put my arms around him and hold him as tightly as I could. I'm tall for my age—five-eight—but Dad's over six feet and I was sorry I wasn't tall enough to put his head on my shoulder and hold it and let him cry on me. But I put my arms around his waist and burrowed my head against his chest and I could hear his heart and suddenly I was so afraid that one day his heart would stop and then what would I do and I don't know when I realized that, when I became aware, when I, well, when I felt this hardness against my stomach and I didn't know what it was at first and then I knew, I just knew, and I didn't know what to do, whether I should move away or what, and just then Dad put his arms around me and held me tightly against him and so I figured he didn't want me to move, that it was all right for me to stay there. I just stood real still and it seemed like *it* was getting harder and I couldn't believe I was making that happen but I was! It was me he was holding against him like he didn't want to let go. I mean, I hadn't done anything, not on purpose or anything, and not like I knew it was going to happen, but it was my body pressing against his, my arms around him. It was like I had this power. Older boys had started looking at me. Whenever I went over to the college or to Dad's office in town to get a ride home, the college boys would want to talk to me and they couldn't believe it when I told them I was only fourteen. I knew it was my breasts that boys liked, but I didn't really understand until that Sunday that I have a power over men because I'm a woman, and there isn't much they can do about it. Not even my own father.

We didn't stand there long before it was like Dad kind of woke up or something, because suddenly he took his arms from around me, stepped back, and looked toward the door as if he was afraid Rachel might be standing there or about to walk in. His face was red and I saw little tiny beads of sweat on his forehead.

"I need to clean the kitchen," he said, his voice soft and kind of hoarse.

"I'll help you," I offered.

He shook his head. "No. No. I need to be by myself."

"Are you okay?"

He smiled weakly. "I'm fine, sweetheart. I'm fine."

I think he felt kind of weird about what had just happened. I know I did. It was kind of nice but it was also really gross, so I wasn't sorry that he wanted to be alone. I went up to my room and lay on the bed and thought about being named for a dead girl. If I was named for her, who was I supposed to be? Was I me, or was I partly her? But the more I thought about it, and I thought about it a lot, I still do, I realized that all the love my father had for her was now mine, plus all the love he had for me. And maybe all the love, too, he couldn't give to Mom anymore because she didn't seem to want it.

Karen must be home because I hear the front door open and now, footsteps on the stairs. I look at my watch. It's two. What is she doing here? Has something else happened? I stick my head out the door of my room and Karen is coming along the hallway toward me. I rush to her and put my arms around her and hug her tightly. She hugs me back.

"What're you doing here?" I ask. "Why aren't you at work?"

"Have you eaten?" she asks, ignoring my questions.

"No, but I'm not hungry."

"I know," she responds, taking my hand and leading me downstairs. "But your body needs the nutrients whether you want to eat or not. What about some yogurt?"

"That'd be okay."

It's only when we're sitting in the breakfast room and I have almost finished a second carton of blueberry yogurt that I notice how tired Karen looks. "Did you sleep last night?" I ask.

She shakes her head. "I guess I must have slept a couple of hours, but it doesn't feel like it. I look like hell, don't I?"

I nod, smiling.

She smiles back, weakly. "I feel like hell and everybody at the college can see it. They were surprised I came in today, but when the school's chief psychologist shoots his wife in broad daylight, it makes the parents and alumni a little nervous. The worst P.R. job in the world is what they call damage control, and when the damage was done by your ex-husband, it makes things even more difficult. But things seem to be more under control and the president told me I could leave early. Have you seen the papers or watched any television?"

I shake my head.

"I'm glad. It's front page of the *New York Times, Boston Globe, Washington Post,* and every other newspaper in the country, and it's the lead item on every network news show."

"So, it's really true, huh? I mean, it wouldn't be in the paper and on television if it wasn't true, would it?" Even as I am thinking that I am not going to cry, the tears start running down my face and the knot in my stomach rips apart and a hole opens up. "My mom's really dead, isn't she?"

"I'm afraid so. I'm really sorry," Karen says softly.

I put the spoon into the yogurt carton and it tips over. I know I should set it upright but all I can do is stare as the tears drop onto the oak table and Karen comes to put her arms around me.

Jeremy

Wednesday Evening
HOME

My grandparents are here. I guess I must have cried myself to sleep on the couch in Mom's studio. I don't remember falling asleep, but I woke up when I heard a car in the driveway. I went downstairs and looked through the window in the door. It was Karen and Jenna. Not long after that, Grandfather Eric drove up in a car, and a little later, Grampy and Gran came.

Grandfather Eric lives in Pennsylvania. Grampy and Gran live in California. Grandfather Eric isn't married anymore. Grandmother Dorothy died when I was little. I don't remember her very well. Grandfather Eric is tall like Dad. I'm probably going to be tall, too. But Grandfather Eric's shoulders are round and he looks like he's bent over, even though he's not. Dad said he got that way after Grandmother Dorothy died. I wonder if that's what happens to you when somebody you love dies.

Grandfather Eric used to be a psychiatrist. That's different than a psychologist, which is what Dad is. Grampy is a lawyer, but he's retired like Grandfather Eric. Grandfather Eric's hair is white. Grampy doesn't have any hair except for his bushy white mustache. Gran kept hugging me and Jenna and calling us "poor things," which I didn't like.

Now, there are a lot of people in the house—Mrs. Allison and some of the other neighbors, and kids from my and Jenna's homerooms and their parents, and Mrs. Worthing, Mr. Zweig, and Jenna's teachers, who I don't know. I keep looking for Miss Albright but she isn't here.

Evan came and so did Jamie Phillips. He's over in a corner with some boys and she's over in another corner with some girls and I'm over here by the door to the kitchen because nobody knows what to say to me and I don't know what to say to them. Everybody keeps telling me that they are sorry and I want to tell them that they aren't half as sorry as I am. It's not fair that all the other kids have a mom and a dad and I don't.

People brought food, more food than we can eat in a month even if we were hungry. I want to go back out to the studio, or just disappear to a place where you can make things unhappen. It would be so cool if there was a place like that.

Maybe if I knew what I was supposed to do it would be all right. Jenna has Karen. They are standing by the fireplace. A bunch of kids from Jenna's school are standing around her and Karen in a semicircle, and I can tell that Jenna's playing one of her roles, because she's talking a lot and fluttering her eyelashes.

Grampy and Gran are standing by the stairs talking to some adults, and Grandfather Eric is by the front door talking to Mrs. Allison. I wish I knew what they were saying, because I don't know what to say to anybody about anything.

The door opens. It's Miss Albright! She closes the door and then looks around like she's looking for somebody. Maybe she's looking for me and I wonder if I should wave my hand and shout, "Over here!" but what if she's *not* looking for me? But I keep staring at her, and finally her eyes find mine and she smiles. She starts across the room toward me, but I hurry to her and throw my arms around her waist and she puts her arms around me. When we stop hugging, I look up at her. There are tears in her eyes. That's better than her saying she's sorry.

"When is the last time you had something to eat?" Miss Albright wants to know.

I can't remember.

She holds out her hand. I take it and we go in the kitchen. The table and counter are filled with plastic containers and dishes covered with plastic wrap. "Ah!" Miss Albright exclaims. "How about a piece of chocolate cake?"

I'm not sure she's serious until I see her take the wrap from around a cake. "Silverware is in the drawer at the end of the counter," I say, pointing.

She has just finished cutting two slices and putting them on plates when I hear a voice say, "Oh, he needs something more nourishing than that." It's Gran. Grampy is with her. "And who might you be, might I ask?"

"Rhoda Albright. I'm one of Jeremy's teachers."

"I see. Well, it's awfully nice of you to stop by, dear, but people are starting to leave and I believe the family needs to be alone now."

"She's my friend!" I blurt out. "She's my friend!" Dad didn't like Gran, because she tries to boss everybody. Mom wasn't crazy about her, either, and she would fight with Gran the way Jenna fought with her. I like Gran. Being bossy is just her way. She doesn't mean anything by it.

"Let the child alone," Grampy says quietly, taking Gran by the elbow and leading her out of the kitchen.

I'm afraid now that Miss Albright will want to leave. But she's not acting like it.

"I'm sorry," I say as she clears some food from the table so we'll have a place to eat our cake. When Miss Albright sits down she doesn't know that she's sitting in Mom's chair. "Gran didn't mean anything."

"I know." Miss Albright is smiling.

"How?"

"I remember what it was like when *my* mother died. I was around your age."

"Really?"

She nods.

"What happened to your mom?" I want to know.

"She had cancer."

"How—how did you feel?"

"Pretty scared and alone. I had two sisters and a brother and my father, but I remember adults talking about us like we couldn't hear and like we didn't have feelings and thoughts about what should happen to us. They wanted to split us up and have us go live with different relatives, because nobody was sure our dad could take care of us by himself. The four of us got together and decided we were going to stay with Dad."

"And what happened?"

"We stayed together and we made it." Miss Albright smiles that smile that makes me feel happy even though I'm sad.

Just then I hear yelling from the family room. It's Jenna and Gran! I hurry into the room just as Jenna screams, "I am not going to live with you in California and I am not going to live with you in Pennsylvania, and neither is Jeremy! We're going to live with Karen!" She's standing by the front door with a bunch of clothes over her arms. Karen stands next to her, her arms full of clothes, too.

Jenna looks at me as if she isn't sure she said the right thing by mentioning my name. I give her a look only she understands, which says I'm glad she stuck up for me, too, even though I'm not sure about the living with Karen part. Dad was right. He said brothers and sisters were closer than husbands and wives because me and Jenna are a hundred percent blood relatives. We share something he and Mom don't. That's why me and Jenna understand each other without having to say a word sometimes and why I can call her "turd face" and she can call me "fart breath" and it's okay.

Gran knows better than to argue with Jenna, especially now. No telling what Jen might do. "Well, perhaps your brother will come to live with us in San Francisco. What about it, Jeremy?"

She turns and gives me a fake smile.

"Or he could come and live with me," Grandfather Eric puts in.

I am holding Miss Albright's hand and she gives mine a little squeeze. I guess I have to be like Jen and like Miss Albright and her brothers and sisters.

"I'm going to live in Mom's studio," I say. I hadn't thought about it before. It just came out and when I heard it, I realized that that's really what I want to do. I don't want to go anywhere. I want to be with Mom. I wish I had thought of it before. Then I could've talked to Jenna about it and maybe she would've stayed here instead of going to Karen's.

Maybe Miss Albright can come and stay here. But she probably has a husband or a boyfriend, so that wouldn't work. But none of that matters. Before my grandparents can start arguing with me, I take Miss Albright upstairs to help me pack my stuff and carry it to the studio.

Miss Albright gets my shirts and pants out of the closet and folds them neatly. I feel a little funny when she opens the dresser drawer and starts taking out my underwear, but she doesn't seem to mind so I don't say anything. I go in Mom and Dad's room and take Dad's suitcase from his closet and Miss Albright puts my clothes in it.

When I come down the stairs lugging the suitcase, Grandfather Eric gets up from the armchair by the fireplace. "Here, son. Let me help you with that."

"That's okay. I've got it," I answer, even though it's way too heavy for me. But since I'm going to be alone from now on, I have to start doing everything for myself.

"Well, all right," he says. "At least put it down a minute. The Pierces and I have been talking and we've decided to go along with you and Jenna's plans for now. Jenna can live with Karen and I'll move here and you can live in your mother's studio if you want. I'll cook your meals and take care of things. I want to be here for Eric's trial anyway."

"What trial?" Grampy says angrily, jumping up from the couch in front of the dead fireplace where he's been sitting with Gran. "You're not going to tell me he's going to plead temporary insanity or some bullshit like that. He shot my daughter in cold blood. Why th' hell do we need a trial?" And he starts crying.

Grandfather Eric doesn't know what to say or do and I sure don't, so when he moves to pick up my suitcase, I let him. Miss Albright is carrying a lot of stuff in her arms.

I open the door to Mom's studio and take the suitcase from Grandfather Eric.

"Thanks," I tell him. I stand in the doorway so he won't come in.

"Well, good night," he says, like he doesn't want to go back in the house.

"G'night," I say. I don't move until he starts back to the house. Then I ask Miss Albright to come in.

I show her around the downstairs part and point to upstairs. "That's where Mom did her drawing and painting." But I don't take her up.

"I liked your mother's work," she says.

"You did?"

"Yes. Whenever we saw each other in town or somewhere, we would chat for a little while about what she was working on, what I was working on. I ran into her shopping at SaveWell about a month ago, and we chatted about having an exhibition of women painters from the area. She was really excited and so was I. I couldn't believe that I was going to get the chance to work with Rachel Pierce!"

It's nice being with someone who misses Mom, too. I'm trying hard to think of something to say so Miss Albright will stay longer but I can't and she says she has to go.

She gives me another hug and I give her one. I stand at the door and watch her walk across the yard and down the driveway to the street where her car is. She pulls her car into the driveway to turn around and blinks her car lights twice, as if she knows I'm looking. I wave back.

Jenna

Friday

"I don't want to go to the funeral home," I tell Karen. It's late morning. Karen took the day off from work and we're sitting in the kitchen. She's on her third cup of coffee. I'm having a can of Coke. "I think it's perverted to call it a *home*. Like it's someplace warm and cozy. And anyway, it's not a *home* for funerals. It's a place for dead people and I'm not into dead people, if you know what I mean. I want to remember Mom as she was when she was alive."

Hearing myself say it, I know I sound stupid. I mean, nobody's *into* dead people. Except undertakers. But tonight is calling hours and people can come and look at Mom's body and we are supposed to be there to greet them. Gross!

"If you don't, you'll regret if for the rest of your life," Karen says in her deep, husky voice, which is even deeper in the morning. She must drive men nuts with that voice. It's perfect for calling people on the phone, like she has to do at her job. I wish mine was like that instead of just ordinary. Karen hasn't put on makeup yet, and I can see dark pouches under her eyes.

"I remember when the dean of students came to my dorm and told me that my parents had been killed in the car accident," she continues. "I didn't believe it. I knew the dean wasn't lying, but it wasn't until I came back here and went to the funeral home and saw them lying there in those two bronze caskets. That's when it really hit me. My parents weren't on vacation and they wouldn't be coming back in a few days, or ever. You have to go, Jenna. Not only for yourself but for your grandparents."

"I wish my grandparents would stay out of it!" I explode. "I mean, I know it's their daughter, but they seem to forget that it's *our* mom. Gran has been making all these decisions about the funeral as if Jeremy and I don't have any feelings. If it was left to me, there wouldn't be a funeral or anything. Just dig a hole in the ground and put the casket in. Mom didn't like a lot of ceremony. A pair of blue jeans and a shirt and she was happy. Gran never understood that about Mom."

Not only don't I want to look at Mom's body, I really don't want to have to deal with talking to a lot of people. About three summers ago a kid in my class drowned in his backyard pool. The school contacted everybody who was in his class and asked us to go by the funeral home at calling hours, that it would mean a lot to his parents. God, was that creepy! You walked in and there was this guy in a dark suit standing right inside the door who made the Addams Family look normal. He said good evening in this voice that made me think of dead flowers and directed us to a room. You turned to go in the room and wham! Right there in front of you was the casket and Brian, that was his name, lying in it like he was asleep. To the right of the casket stood his parents and his brothers and sisters, and you shook hands with each of them and they mumbled something about how glad they were you had come and you mumbled something back about how sorry you were and then after you shook the last hand, there you were at the casket. I guess you were supposed to stand there and look at Brian and get teary or something. I hardly knew him and, frankly, thought he was a bit of a dork, and if I hadn't paid any attention to him when he was alive, why should I pay attention to him now that he was dead? I mean, that would've been insincere. So after I shook his little sister's hand, I breezed past that casket like it was filled with snakes and headed toward the other side of the room where there was a table set up with punch and cookies, and for the whole rest of the miserable time I was there, which wasn't more than a half hour, I stood with my back to the casket. But tonight I'm the one who's supposed to thank people for coming to stare at my mom.

"Well, fine!" I announce. "If I am going to be on public display, then I need something to wear, not only for calling hours tonight but for the funeral tomorrow. Everybody is going to be looking at me, especially the girls. They'll be hoping I look a wreck and I don't want to give them the satisfaction. It's sick, I know, but girls are like that. Me included."

Karen shakes her head, laughing quietly. "I figured you might say something like that, which is why I took the day off. What do you say we go over to the mall in Summerton and go to Bloomingdale's?"

"Bloomingdale's!" I shout. "God, Karen. You are just too cool."

I rush upstairs, get dressed, put on makeup, and off we go. When I grow up I want to live in Bloomingdale's or maybe Nordstrom. We don't have a Nordstrom here, but Gran took me to the one in San Francisco and let me buy everything I wanted and didn't even blink when the total came to almost a thousand dollars. It's more fun to shop when you don't have to look at the price tags. Gran will be pleased I went to the trouble to make a good personal appearance. I'm sure she'll be happy to pay Karen back.

It takes me a while to decide, but I finally settle on stockings and a really nice pair of black shoes with a low heel and a square buckle to go with a gray wool dress that has a scoop neck and falls just below my knees. However, once I have it on with the shoes and stockings, it's obvious that the stockings don't work. I look like a long-legged kid playing dress-up. But what about white stockings! They will set off both the dress and my legs very nicely and give me a vulnerable look. But is that really what I want? There's a thin line between looking vulnerable and people feeling sorry for you. And I couldn't stand it if people started feeling sorry for me.

A shawl! A white Irish-knit shawl. I'll look vulnerable but the shawl will also make me look in control, too. And it'll give me something to do with my hands, because shawls are always slipping off your shoulders.

When I get everything together, I model it for Karen.

"Very nice," she says admiringly. "What about the funeral tomorrow? You should wear black."

"Black works best when it's in leather and even *I* wouldn't wear a black leather dress to a funeral," I say as I head to the dressing room to change, Karen's laughter following me.

I know that I want to look all business tomorrow, and after trying on several outfits, I decide on a gray suit and a dark red blouse. It's somber but not sad, and the blouse gives a dignified splash of color.

While Karen's paying for everything, I see a nice pair of pumps that match the blouse perfectly and we get them. The only other thing is what to do with my hair. I think I'll wear it down tonight and put it in a bun tomorrow.

I feel superficial spending all this time thinking about clothes and what kind of impression I'm going to make. But maybe I *am* superficial. And having to shop gave me something else to think about.

It's going on four when Karen and I get back to her house. Calling hours start at six. I hurry upstairs to my room and as I take off my sweater and blouse, my fingers brush against my navel ring. I play with it idly for a second, then continue undressing. I stand naked in front of the full-length mirror on the back of the door and look at the rings, the one in my navel and the one in my right nipple.

Mom and I never talked about it, but it wasn't the navel ring that pissed her off. I had on a tank top that evening and I was real eager to get home, go upstairs, and put on a blouse, because the tank top was pressing against my breast and my nipple was hurting like hell. All I was thinking about was putting on something that wouldn't be pressing on my breasts and taking a couple of aspirin. I didn't even think about Rachel, because I just knew she would be in the studio. So I was totally unprepared when I came tearing in the back door and she was in the kitchen.

"Oh, hi, Mom!" I said in that fake cheery voice kids pull out when they've been caught doing something they knew they shouldn't have.

"Hi, honey," Dad said to Mom, coming in behind me. I could tell that he had wanted to sneak in, too, because his voice was so high he was chirping. He sounded more phony than I did.

Mom didn't say a word. She saw the navel ring first. How

could she not, since I was naked from below my tits to my hips? Her mouth dropped open. Then I saw her eyes move up. I think they were headed to my face but they stopped at my breasts. I was hoping she wouldn't see it, but later, when I got up to my room and looked in the mirror, the nipple ring was pressed against the yellow top and you had to be blind or a little kid like Jeremy not to see it.

What had I been thinking about? It wasn't like Dad and I had planned on it when we left the house that afternoon. We were driving through Old Town in Summerton, where all the artists and New Age people have shops, and I saw this sign that said PIERCINGS and I mentioned how cool I thought it would be to get one. I was talking more to myself, so I was surprised when Dad asked me what part of my body I would get pierced if I ever did it. Without even thinking, I said maybe my navel or my nipple. I felt kind of weird saying that to my own father, even though he made a point of explaining all about sex to me when I was nine or ten and always let me know I could talk to him about anything. But still, *nipple* was not a word you say to your dad so I was totally unprepared when he said I could get pierced if I wanted to.

Oh, man! I didn't know what to think or what to say. I wasn't even sure I wanted a piercing. I still remembered getting my ears pierced when I was seven and that burned like somebody had set my earlobes on fire. But if I said no, I was afraid Dad might think I was just a lot of talk. *I* might think I was a lot of talk. Then I thought about the reaction of the girls at school when I undressed in the locker room for gym class. They would shit! That's when I said sure.

Mom went ballistic and started screaming and yelling about how she didn't appreciate not being consulted, and when Dad tried to explain that it had been his idea and it was just a spur-of-the-moment thing, that made it worse. The angrier Mom got, the cooler Dad got. That's how he is. Maybe it's from being a psychologist. I don't know, but whenever anybody gets real emotional, he is just cool and calm. Finally he very quietly explained to Rachel that she was overreacting like she always did when she was PMS and did she want him to get the Pamprin for her and Mom hit him so hard he staggered and tears came into his eyes. Even though I agreed with Dad about Mom overreacting, that little PMS remark pissed *me* off.

It takes me a little while to get the rings out of my navel and nipple, but I finally do. I throw them on top of the dresser, then hurry and get dressed.

It's a little after five when Karen and I get to the funeral home. The same creepy guy who was at the door when they had the calling hours for Brian is here tonight. I expect to be ushered toward the room where Brian was, but he leads us down the hallway to the back and into a large room. Jeremy is already here with Miss Albright. He is standing in front of the casket, blocking my view, which is fine with me.

Gran and Grampy come in from across the hall. She looks almost happy, as if she is hostessing the dinner party before a debutante ball.

"Jenna! You look lovely, dear!" she exclaims, her face beaming. "The shawl is a lovely touch, just lovely."

"Thank you, Grandmother. I hoped you'd be pleased. Karen took me to Bloomingdale's today to get things for tonight and tomorrow."

As I had hoped, she turns to Karen and says, "That was very thoughtful of you, dear. You've done so much for Jenna. I certainly don't expect you to pay for her expensive taste in clothes. How much did you have to spend?"

Karen whispers something to Gran, who calls Grampy over. He goes away and a couple of moments later comes back and gives Karen a check. Cool! My grandparents flutter out of the room and across the hall, where the caterer they hired is setting up the refreshments.

I really don't want to be here. I still have my back to the casket and just when I think I can escape having to look in it, I feel someone take my hand. It's Karen, and before I can say or do anything, she has turned me around and we're walking toward the casket. Jeremy's standing to the side now, holding Miss Albright's hand.

"Hey, fart breath," I greet him, still not looking at Mom.

"Turd face." He smiles at me weakly.

"How you doing?"

He shrugs. "How're you doing?"

"Yeah. Like that."

Taking a deep breath, I look down, expecting to see Mom. Instead, there's something that looks like it's from the wax museum Grampy took us to the last time we were in San Francisco. The thing in the casket kind of resembles Mom, but it's wearing a dark blue suit, a white blouse, and makeup. This is the first time in my life I've seen her in a suit and makeup. I don't think Mom even owns one! Looks like Gran has been to Bloomingdale's, too. God, Mom must be pissed!

There's a lot of powder on her face and it makes her look like an undercooked pastry that's been sprinkled with too much confectioners' sugar. There's rouge on her cheeks and a bright red garish lipstick on her mouth. Gross! Really gross!

I let go of Karen's hand and start to turn away when something catches my eye. I turn back and notice a little shiny place on Mom's forehead. I see another one beneath her right eye. It's like somebody took a piece of plastic or something and pressed it on her face. Then I realize what those shiny places are and I feel a scream about to burst from my body. But I am afraid to let it, afraid it will tear down all the walls of every building in every country in the world, so I ball my hand into a fist and put it in my mouth and blackness rises up like a giant wave and swallows me as I slump to the floor next to Mom's casket.

Leather. My hand is touching leather. I open my eyes slowly. It seems that I'm lying on a leather couch. Where am I? How did I get here? Something is squeezing my other hand so tightly it hurts. I turn my head. It's Jeremy. He looks like he's been crying.

"Hey, fart breath," I whisper weakly.

He grins and lunges atop me and gives me a hug so tight it's hard to breathe.

"Lighten up," I tell him. "I love you, too."

He lets go and moves back, still grinning. I sit up slowly and look around. Gran and Grampy, Karen, Miss Albright, and a man who looks like the creepy guy at the door, only older, are staring at me, looking worried. "Hi," I say, and try to smile. "What happened?"

"You—you were looking at your mother and suddenly you put a fist in your mouth and fainted," Karen says. "You haven't been out long, but we were just about to call an ambulance."

"No, no. I'm okay now." I remember what happened, and remembering, I feel like I may faint again. Instead, tears come into my eyes.

"What happened?" Karen continues.

The man hands me a box of tissue. He must be Mr. Wilson, the funeral director, and this must be his office. As I take the box from him, I say, "The shiny patches on her forehead and beneath her right eye."

He turns red and looks very uncomfortable.

"What are you talking about, dear?" Gran asks.

"Is—is that where the bullet holes were?" I ask, still looking at the man I think is Mr. Wilson. I can't believe how calm I am. Like Dad.

His mouth opens as if he doesn't know what to say or if he even has a voice. He looks from me to my grandparents to Karen, his face a plea.

"It's all right, Mr. Wilson," Karen says in her soft, deep voice. "Her mother taught her to be very observant. You can answer her question."

Mr. Wilson turns back to me and clears his throat. "I'm sorry, Miss Richards. I truly am. We did our best. But we had to reconstruct most of the face from photographs. She had a very fine, very delicate bone structure. We tried our best to make her look presentable."

Miss Richards. No one has ever called me that. And he looked at me the entire time he was talking. I was the one who wanted to know. I was the one who needed an answer. And he spoke to *me*, not Karen or even my grandmother.

"You did a good job," I tell him. I hear him breathe a sigh of relief. I wonder if he was scared I was going to blame him for something or want to sue him. I stand up slowly and gather the shawl around my shoulders. "You did a fine job, Mr. Wilson, but I don't think my mother would want anyone else to see her. Would you mind closing the casket before the people start arriving?"

"But she looks lovely!" Gran exclaims. "Jenna, dear. You're just upset. I know it's hard for you to understand, but you are not the only one whose feelings matter here."

I am just about to start screaming at her like Mom used to do when Mr. Wilson turns to Gran and says, "Ma'am. Begging your pardon, but I believe Miss Richards is right. While I am proud of the work we did, I used to see Miss Pierce walk past here every morning on her way to DiCarlo's. She was so beautiful and so filled with life. I used to look at her and be glad that I would not have to prepare her body for burial. Such passion and liveliness as hers should never die, I used to think. And now it has. I don't think she would want anyone to see her. I should also tell you, ma'am, it is our policy not to open caskets for viewing when the deceased has been subjected to a terrible trauma. I did so only at your insistence, ma'am."

The room is silent. I look at Mr. Wilson and am sorry I was so quick to judge him and his son. It takes guts to stand up to my grandmother. I wonder if Mom had to stand up to her before she could be an artist. But who knows? If she hadn't, she might still be alive. That's probably what Gran thinks. Well, I don't care. All I know is that if Gran says no to Mr. Wilson, I'll close the casket myself.

No one seems to know what to do or say. I become aware of Jeremy. He is holding Miss Albright's hand and looking seriously from me to Mr. Wilson and to Gran. Without thinking, I say, "Jeremy? What do you think?" After the words are out of my mouth, I am sorry. What if he wants the casket open?

Without hesitating he says, in a strong, clear voice, "I think our mom has been hurt enough."

I can't believe he said that. I look at him as if seeing him for the first time. I mean, I've always thought of him as being a little dorky, of being a mama's boy, even if he is my brother, but dorky or not, I am beginning to think he just might be a pretty cool little person.

"The children are right," Grampy says.

It's four against one, if I count Mr. Wilson. He doesn't wait to hear if Gran is going to agree but hurries out of his office and down the hall to the room where Mom's casket is.

Grampy looks at his watch. "It's five to six. It's time." He takes Gran's arm and they walk out slowly. Jeremy, Miss Albright, Karen, and I follow.

I feel a little weak but I'm okay. When we go into the room, the casket is closed. Mr. Wilson tells us to stand at a right angle to the casket so that when people come in the door they will shake each of our hands first.

"Miss Richards, you will be first in the receiving line since you are the oldest child. Young Mr. Richards will be next, and Mr. and Mrs. Pierce will come next."

"What about Karen?" I want to know. She has been standing next to me.

"And Miss Albright?" Jeremy puts in anxiously. Miss Albright is going to need a new hand after tonight, because Jeremy is going to squeeze that one until it falls off.

"We're not family," Karen says.

"Yes, you are!" I protest, afraid that I'll never have a family again.

"We'll be nearby if you need us," Miss Albright reassures us, and retrieves her hand from Jeremy. She gives him a hug and moves away.

I go into the hall to see if any people are waiting to come in. I can't believe my eyes. "Jeremy! Come here!"

Through the glass doors we see that the front porch is filled. We run across the hall to the room where the food is set up and look out the window. "Look, Jeremy!" People are lined up all the way down the street for what must be a couple of blocks. I can't believe it!

We hurry back across the hall and get in line just as Mr. Wilson opens the front door.

Calling hours are supposed to end at eight, but eight o'clock comes and goes and people are still coming. I recognize very few faces, but as each person shakes my hand and Jeremy's, they say almost the same thing: "Your mother was a very special person and I'm going to miss her." Many of them are carrying flowers, which they leave on top of the casket. Others are carrying cards and drawings, which they put on the floor in front of the casket.

It is almost ten o'clock when the last person leaves. Part of me is really, really happy. So many people and they all loved my mother and came to tell us. I wish I had known the person they were talking about. I didn't get to sit with Mom at the table in the window at DiCarlo's and talk about what was in the paper or whatever she and all these people who knew her talked about. And now I never will. Now I never will.

Jeremy

Sunday Night
KAREN'S HOUSE

It's dark! I sit up in bed and I don't know where I am. I don't even know which way to turn to get out of bed. Then I see light beneath the door and I remember: I am at Karen's and my mother is dead.

The funeral was today. The church was packed. Even the balcony was full. Neither me nor Jenna had ever been in a church. It's kind of weird to have your first time in church be at your mother's funeral. Jenna said Mom was friends with the minister of that church and she wanted Mom's funeral to be there.

I was afraid it was going to be real sad. It was and it wasn't. A lot of people got up and talked about Mom and told stories about her—people from the college, people from the bookstore in town she liked to go to, some politicians, and a couple of people from New York who had something to do with art. My mom was an important person and I didn't even know it. All those people in the church knew my mother and I didn't know who hardly any of them were. I had no idea so many people loved my mom. People seemed happy they had known her and it made me proud that I'm her son. When I grow up I hope people will be happy they know me.

The hard part was having to sit in the front and look at the casket. It was so close to us that I almost could have touched it. It was hard to believe my mother was inside and that I would never be this close to her ever again.

Then all the talking and singing was over and men came and put Mom's casket on their shoulders and walked up the center aisle of the church and me and Jen followed them and everybody was standing and watching and I grabbed Jen's hand and held it tight and she squeezed mine really hard and it hurt but that was okay. They slid Mom's casket into the hearse and we got in the limousine that was parked right behind it, me, Jen, and Gran and Grampy, who was making little noises like a puppy whimpering to be let in the house.

As the hearse began to move away from the church, it was like there were two me's—one was sitting in the limousine dressed in a dark suit, a white shirt, and a black tie, but the *real* me was off somewhere else and I kept hoping that the real me would come back and I would wake up and tell Mom about the weird dream I'd had about going to her funeral.

There was a police car in front of the hearse and it led us slowly through town. Looking out the window, I could see people stopping to watch as we passed and it was like everybody knew whose funeral it was. Some people made that funny motion with their hand where they touch their forehead, chest, and shoulders. I've seen people on TV shows do it. It has a name but I forget what it is. It looked kind of cool, though. We drove past Sutter's and then the college and then out to South Birchfield and the cemetery near our house.

When we got to the cemetery, it was supposed to be just me, Jenna, Gran, and Grampy, because the minister had made an announcement at church that the family wanted the burial to be private but that we would be receiving people at our house afterward. That was the first me and Jen knew about that. We looked at each other and we didn't even have to say anything. Karen and Miss Albright were sitting behind us, and we both turned around and asked them if they would come to the cemetery with us. So they were there, too, along with Reverend Edwards and the men from the funeral home. It was another sunny day. The sun has been shining bright every day since Mom died.

Some men from the funeral home were waiting at the cemetery and they took Mom's casket out of the hearse and we followed as they carried it up the hill. I think I was doing okay until we got close to the top and I saw the rectangular hole and a big pile of dirt beside it. Jen and I were squeezing each other's hands really hard. Reverend Edwards read some words from a book but I didn't really hear what she said. I just kept looking at Mom's casket and thinking that I was never ever going to see her again, not even if I live to be a hundred.

Then the men picked up the casket. There were some kind of straps over the grave and while two men put the casket on the straps, four men held the straps real tight and when the casket was set on it they started letting it down slowly into the grave. That's when I started crying. Jenna really lost it. And she wasn't *emoting*. We hugged each other real hard and probably got snot on each other's clothes but that was okay.

When the men pulled the straps up, Gran motioned to us. We managed to stop crying and followed her to the pile of dirt. She told us to take a handful and throw it in the grave. The dirt was cold like snow. The handful I grasped had a rock in it and I put it back. I couldn't throw a rock on Mom. I grabbed another handful and this one didn't have any rocks in it. Jen and I went to the edge of the grave and dropped our dirt in. It made a dull sound when it hit the casket, like a bell trying to ring when it's broken. Then Gran and Grampy dropped their dirt in. Grampy was crying real hard and loud now. Karen and Miss Albright dropped a handful of dirt in. We stood there for a while and nobody said anything. I looked around for Dad. Last night after calling hours were over I overheard Grampy tell Karen that Dad's lawyer had said some guards could bring Dad to the cemetery today if it was all right with the family. Grampy said if Dad came near Mom's grave he'd kill him. That would be all right with me.

Finally, we started walking down the hill, me and Jen, then Karen and Miss Albright, and our grandparents and Reverend Edwards.

I wanted to go home and fall asleep in the studio, but Grandfather Eric had gone back to Pennsylvania to do some stuff so he could move here to stay with me. After Grampy yelled at him about Dad and all, he probably figured it was best if he disappeared until after the funeral. But even if he had been here, I couldn't have gone to the house, because of all the people who'd be there.

When we got back to the roadway where the limousine was parked, Karen's car and Miss Albright's were behind it. Jenna went and got in Karen's car and I went to Miss Albright's. Gran rushed over to Karen and her mouth was moving real fast like she was angry about something, but Karen hugged her and Gran stopped talking and started crying and Karen was whispering in her ear. I don't know what she said but whatever it was, Gran stopped crying after a minute, took some rumpled tissue from her pocketbook and blew her nose, then went and got in the limousine, where Grampy was, and drove away. Miss Albright took me to Karen's.

Karen made hot chocolate from scratch. That's the way Mom always made it. We sat around the kitchen—she has a big round oak table like we do—but none of us felt like talking. And that was okay since none of us knew what to say, anyway. It was just nice sitting there with Karen and Miss Albright and Jenna.

When we were almost done with our chocolate, Miss Albright got up to go. I walked her to the front door, where I gave her a big hug, thanked her, and let her out. When I got back to the kitchen I noticed how pale Jen was looking and I went and sat beside her at the table and held her hand.

"You looked really pretty today," I said.

She smiled then and gave me a little kiss on the cheek. I blushed.

Karen suggested we take a nap and without a word, we headed upstairs. I knew I was tired but I didn't think I'd sleep until night, but the numbers on the clock radio by the bed say it's seven o'clock! I get out of bed and open the door to the hallway so the light will come in. I find my shoes under the bed, put them on, and go downstairs, where I hear Karen's low voice coming from the kitchen.

"Hi!" I greet her and Jen, who are sitting at the table.

Jenna yawns. "Hi, yourself."

"Did you just wake up, too?"

She nods. "About a half hour ago."

"We slept over four hours!" I exclaim.

Jenna giggles. "You want to put a twenty in front of that four?"

"What do you mean? Hey! You mean we slept *twenty-four* hours? No way!"

Karen smiles. "It's Sunday night."

"No way!" I repeat.

"Karen tricked us. She got something from her doctor and put it in our hot chocolate."

"You both needed the sleep and so did I."

I can't believe I slept so long. I wonder if that's what it's like for Mom now, except she won't wake up. I plop down in a chair next to Jen.

"Why don't I call out for pizza?" Karen suggests.

"Cool!" Jen and I respond together, and break out laughing.

"What do you like on it?"

"Hamburger!" I say.

"Mushrooms and anchovies," says Jen.

"Yuck!" I respond.

"Okay. We'll get two pizzas, well, three, since I like mine with green peppers and onions."

Karen picks up her cell phone, which is on the table, and calls the pizzeria. When she's done, she looks at me and says, "Jenna and I had just started talking about tomorrow. It's a school day, you know."

"Oh."

"I was thinking about that at the funeral yesterday," Jen says. "When it happened, I swore I'd never go back to school, but now I don't mind as much as I thought I would. It's like everything stood still until the funeral, like a freeze-frame in a movie. Now the projector can start rolling again. Going to school will give me something to do. I'm tired of thinking and I'm really tired of feeling."

"I wish people would pretend like nothing ever happened," I put in.

"Fat chance of that," Jenna says.

"I wouldn't worry," Karen says. "After tomorrow that's probably how it'll be."

"So what's going to happen to us?" Jenna asks. "I mean, like, after school is out next year. What's going to happen to us? And the house? What about the house?"

"And all Mom's paintings?" I add.

"Well, your grandparents and I talked," Karen answers. "As you probably know, they think you should go live with them in San Francisco immediately."

"Was Gran mad because we didn't go back to the house after the funeral?" I want to know. "What did you say to her?"

"Just that the two of you were very tired and needed to get some sleep. She understood. She needs to be with people who knew Rachel and hear them talk about her. Especially since she and Rachel didn't get along. They hadn't seen or spoken to each other in more than a year."

"I didn't know that," Jen says. "What happened? I mean, why weren't they talking?"

"It was complicated. Rachel and I talked about it, but I'm not sure I really understood. I mean, I was nineteen when my mother died, so it's hard for me to understand when people can't get along with their mothers or their mothers with them. Rachel's death is very hard on your grandmother, especially since it seems like Rachel talked to your grandfather almost every week and your grandmother never knew."

I look at Jen and there are tears in her eyes. I bet she's sorry now that she argued with Mom so much. Everything is real quiet for a minute. It's like we were talking about something but no one remembers. Then I do. "So what's going to happen to us?"

Karen smiles. "Right. I talked with your grandmother on the phone this morning before they left for the airport."

"I don't want to go live with her!" Jenna says emphatically. "I want to stay here!"

"And that's how it's going to be for the remainder of this school year. Then we'll see what's best."

"Is that your way of saying that you don't want me living here next year?" Jenna asks angrily. That's the tone of voice that always sent Mom through the roof, but Karen just smiles.

"Not at all." Her voice is quiet. "If staying here with me is what's best, then that's the way it'll be."

"And who is going to decide what's best?" Jenna wants to know.

"The two of you, your grandparents, and me."

"Well, I'm going to want to stay here!" Jen says in that tone of voice she uses when she doesn't want you to argue with her. "It's like everybody has forgotten about Dad. I mean, I understand and everything, but he's still my dad and we don't really know what happened. You know? I'm sure he has a reason and that he didn't mean to do it."

If she weren't about to start crying, I'd tell her that *I'm* trying *real* hard to forget him. I don't want to ever see him again.

"Grandfather Eric went to see him every day before he went back to Pennsylvania," Jenna says. "I—I wanted to go at first, but now, I don't know. I mean, what would I say, you know? Karen, have—have you seen him?"

She nods slowly. "His lawyer called and said he wanted to see me."

"How is he?" Jenna asks.

"He seems very depressed. We didn't talk long. Neither one of us knew what to say."

"Did he say why he did it?"

"No. He didn't say and I didn't ask."

"What did he want?" I ask.

Karen gets up from the table and goes upstairs. When she comes back, she's carrying a white envelope. "He wanted me to give this to you."

She puts the envelope on the table kind of halfway between me and Jenna. It has both our names on it. We look at it but neither one of us moves to open it.

"Do you know what it says?" Jenna asks.

"No. It was sealed when he gave it to me and I didn't ask."

The envelope just sits there, neither one of us knowing what to do about it. Finally, Jenna pushes it across the table to Karen. "Read it to us."

Karen opens it and reads it to herself first, then,

Dear Jen and Jeremy,

I can certainly understand if you hate me. I hate myself. I know you want to know why, what happened. I wish I knew. I'm sure you must have noticed that Rachel and I had not been getting along for a while. I know you loved your mother very much and I don't want to say anything that would change your opinion of her, but all of this is probably going to come out at the trial. So I'd rather you hear it from me than read it in the newspaper or hear it in the hall in school.

Your mother was going out with another man. I didn't know until she told me that morning, the morning it happened. She told me she was going to leave and take the two of you with her. I suppose I went crazy. She was very angry. You know how angry Rachel could get. I have never seen her as angry as she was that morning. She left the house and I don't know what happened. I must have blacked out or something because the next thing I remember is sitting on the porch at home, holding a gun to my head, and a lot of police around.

Everybody says I am the one who killed her but I have no recollection of that. I am so sorry.

I would like to see you but not yet. I am too ashamed and I don't think I could bear to see you look at me with hate in your eyes, although I deserve your hatred. Despite everything, don't ever forget that I love the two of you more than anything. You're all I have now.

Take care of yourselves. I would love to hear from you.

All my love,
Dad

The doorbell rings.

"That must be the pizza," Karen says. "One of you guys want to come and help me carry the boxes?"

"I will," I say quickly. Jen's head is down. I'm not sure but I think she's crying.

I go to answer the door while Karen hurries upstairs to get her wallet. The pizza guy is holding three of those big red plastic things inside of which are the boxes of pizzas. He unsnaps them and hands me the pizzas. The bottom one is really hot. I rush back to the kitchen with them.

"Man, these pizzas are hot like they just came out of the oven!" I exclaim, dropping them on the table. Jen doesn't look up. "Hey!" I say gently. "What's the matter?"

She looks up and tears are coming down her face. "It just sucks."

"What?"

"Life! What do you think, stupid? Rachel is dead. Dad's in jail. And we're two pathetic orphans."

"Do you believe what Dad said in his letter?" I ask softly.

"About what?"

"About—about Mom, you know, fooling around?"

"Why would he lie? Dad wouldn't lie to us. Not to me, he wouldn't."

"I don't know. He killed Mom, didn't he?"

"Well, you were always a mama's boy."

"So? You were a daddy's girl!"

Tears are still coming down Jen's face but she's mad now and I don't know why.

"What's going on, you two?" Karen asks as she comes in the kitchen.

Neither one of us says anything. Karen goes to a cabinet and gets plates. I get knives and forks from the silverware drawer. Karen sets a plate in front of each of us. "Now, who ordered what?"

"I'm not hungry," Jen announces. "I want to write Dad and tell him how much I love him and that I understand and I'll always love him." She glares at me.

"What're you looking at me for?" I say, my voice rising. "You can believe him if you want to. I don't. I don't think Mom did what he said. I know she didn't!" I am yelling now.

"And how do you know?" Jen shoots back.

"I just do!" We are standing in front of each other. Her face is angry-ugly and probably mine is, too. But I don't care. "And even if she did, he didn't have to kill her," I shout. "Why didn't they just get divorced like everybody else's parents?" I start crying.

"He didn't do it on purpose! He didn't mean to do it!"

"So what? So what, Jenna? She's still dead, isn't she?"

"That's enough," Karen says softly. She steps toward us as if she wants to hug me or Jen or both of us, but I don't want her touching me and I step out of the way.

"I want to go home, Karen. I—I don't want to stay here anymore."

"Go! See if I care!" Jenna spits at me.

"Please, Karen," I whine.

"I'm sorry, Jeremy. You can't."

"But why?" I shout. "I want to go to my house!"

"You know no one's there. Your grandfather Eric won't be back for another few days, maybe a week. You can't stay there by yourself. Sit, Jeremy. Have some pizza before it gets cold."

She knows I hate cold pizza. I sit down slowly and open the boxes until I find the one with hamburger. It's still hot as I take a slice dripping with cheese and grease and put it on my plate.

"What do you want to drink?"

"Coke."

"Coming right up!"

Jenna wipes her eyes. "How can you sit here and stuff your face with pizza after hearing that letter from Dad?"

"I was starting to think you were pretty cool, Jenna, but you're as big a jerk as you always were."

She takes Dad's letter and stomps from the room without saying anything back to me. She must really be mad, because Jenna always gets in the last word.

Jenna

I read Dad's letter over and over. I didn't want to let Jeremy know, but I'm not sure I believe what he said about Mom, either. That doesn't sound like her. I guess I got so angry at Jeremy because I needed him to believe Dad. If Jeremy believed what Dad said about Mom, then it had to be true.

What a fucking soap opera! What am I supposed to do, huh? I don't know whether to cry for my mother or stand up for my father, or cry for him and stand up for my mom. I wish I could disappear like on *Star Trek*. Just transport me out of here and put me down on another planet in a galaxy far, far away, where I don't have to deal with any of this.

I hate him for doing this to us. Jeremy, the little twerp, is right. It's not like Dad had never heard of divorce. It's no big deal anymore. And it's not like he had to be concerned about divorce doing something to me and Jeremy. We were the odd kids in school, anyway, because our parents were still together. Well, he really made us odd now.

I keep trying to see it in my mind, my dad pointing a gun at my mom and pulling the trigger, not once but twice. And I can't do it! And where did he get a gun? It doesn't make sense. Dad was always so calm and in control. He must've flipped out. That's the only thing that makes sense.

But why? What could she have done? I read Dad's letter again, and I stop at the part where he says Mom was going to leave him and take us with her. I don't know. Take Jeremy, for sure. Take me? I kind of doubt it. Mom moved out to the studio so she wouldn't have to live under the same roof with me or Dad. Nothing makes sense. Nothing. Except... I wonder if Mom found out and confronted Dad about it. That's the only reason I can think that she would have taken Jeremy *and* me. Nothing else makes sense. I don't want to think about it. I have to write Dad. But what do I say? Wait. I know. I'll send him a picture. I'll draw a picture of myself and he can put it up on the wall at the jail! That's what I'll do!

Mom never paid much attention to my artwork. Not until the vagina on the bathroom wall. Jeremy was always *the talented one,* and I admit, he's incredible. But I'm no slouch. I have to work at it harder than he does, and who knows? Maybe if I did work at it, maybe if I took it seriously, I'd be as good as him and Mom. Maybe Mom didn't take me seriously because I didn't take myself seriously.

The only paper I have is some lined notebook paper. I guess that'll have to do. I stare at myself in the mirror as if I am somebody else, and I see a girl with a round face that's not thin, but there's still a little baby fat around her cheeks. Her eyes are dark, so dark that they are not a distinct color. Her hair is dark also, and long. Her nose is small and the lips are thin. She's not ugly and she's not pretty, but she's not plain, either.

I sketch quickly, first the oval for the head. I put in some lines to suggest hair and then lightly put in the eyes and nose. It is the mouth that will carry the feeling. I want Dad to not be depressed, so I will make the mouth smile, parting the lips just a tiny bit to show a hint of teeth. It's a sweet smile, a little girl smile but with just a hint that she's really not a little girl anymore.

Jeremy

Monday Morning

When I come downstairs, Jenna's sitting at the table eating cold pizza for breakfast. Serves her right for stomping off last night. She acts like I'm not in the room and doesn't even look at me. I don't care!

But maybe she's scared like I am about going back to school. It's going to be so weird. I feel like some freak—the kid without a mother. I think I hate everybody who has a mother.

Karen's sitting at the table drinking coffee. "Do you want anything to eat?" she asks.

I shake my head. I'm afraid she's going to ask me how I'm feeling or try to get me to talk about my feelings, but she goes back to her coffee. She doesn't even give me a lecture about breakfast being the most important meal of the day and all that crap. She just drinks her coffee like she probably did all the mornings before Jen and I showed up.

Jenna has a notebook on the table and she opens it and takes out a folded piece of paper and gives it to Karen. "Could you see that my dad gets this?"

Karen takes it. "I'll get an envelope to put it in, seal it, and give it to his lawyer."

"Thanks."

I can't believe Jenna wrote him! I can't believe she did that! I hate her! I get up from the table and tear out of the room. I'd rather sit by myself in the living room than be in the same room with her!

A few minutes later Karen comes and tells me it's time to go. She understood without our even having to say anything that neither me nor Jenna wants to ride the bus today. That would be too much. When Karen opens the garage door, I make sure to get in the backseat so I can be away from Jenna.

Jenna will get dropped off first. Her school starts an hour before mine. She usually wears makeup and stuff on her face, but I don't think she put any on today. She's not wearing any of her fancy clothes, either. She has on a big sweater that Mom used to wear. It's white with what look like thick ropes twisted together. Mom said it was an Irish fisherman's sweater. Jenna looks different. Like she's older or something. I wonder if I look older. I sure feel like it.

We drive up to the middle school just as the first bus is pulling in. Jenna gets out of the car but doesn't say good-bye to me and I don't say anything to her. I get in the front seat.

"It's an hour before I drop you off. What do you say I buy you an Egg McMuffin, whether you want it or not?" Karen says as we're driving away.

"Sure." I am feeling a little hungry.

We're almost to town before I ask her, "What did you think of Dad's letter?"

"What do you mean?"

"What he said about Mom? About Mom fooling around?"

Karen is watching the traffic, but I can tell she's trying to figure out what to say. I hate it when adults won't tell you the truth but try to figure out what they think you can understand.

"Tell me the truth," I add. "I don't know what to believe anymore about anything. Do you think my mom was fooling around?"

We are coming up to the light in the center of town and Karen flips on the right turn signal and that way we won't have to go past Sutter's, even though it's shorter to go straight.

"It's okay," I tell her. "I can't spend the rest of my life not going by Sutter's."

"You sure?"

"Yes, I'm sure."

I don't know what I expected to see, but Sutter's looks like it always has. What did I think? That there was going to be blood pouring down the front of the building? If you didn't know what had happened in front of it last week, you couldn't tell by looking at it today. And the only thing that's pouring is sunshine. More sunshine.

"I don't believe your mother was fooling around."

Karen's voice startles me but not as much as what she just said. "You don't?" I ask. "You aren't just saying that, are you, to make me feel better?"

"I wouldn't do that, Jeremy. But you have to promise me something."

"What?"

"Don't tell Jenna I said that."

"Why?"

"I would just prefer that you didn't."

"But why?" I ask, my voice rising.

"Because I'm asking you not to."

"All right," I say grudgingly.

We don't say anything else. When we get to McDonald's she gets me an Egg McMuffin, and another cup of coffee for herself. I'm angry and don't want to talk to her because she won't tell Jenna that Dad is lying.

When it's time to drop me at school, I'm sorry I had something to eat because my stomach is hurting a little.

When we get there, the buses haven't started coming yet and I'm glad. If we had driven up and all the buses were there and Mrs. Worthing was greeting all the kids, I wouldn't have gotten out of the car.

"Are you going to my house after school, or your house?" Karen wants to know. "It's okay if you go there. You just can't stay overnight until your grandfather comes back."

"I'll be in Mom's studio." Otherwise I'll have to ride the school bus to town to get to Karen's and then be stuck in the house with Jenna.

"I'll pick you up after I'm done at work."

"Thanks," I say as I get out of the car. I look across the street to the top of the hill where Mom is. Then I go inside.

Miss Albright's room is the very first one on the right when you come in. My stomach stops hurting when I notice that her door is open and the light's on.

"Hi!" I say, hurrying into the room.

"Oh!" Miss Albright gives a little scream. "Jeremy! You scared me!"

I smile. "What're you doing?"

"Setting up for the day."

"Can I help?"

"Well, sure. Here. Put four boxes of crayons on each table."

"Who're they for?" I want to know.

"Mrs. Tyler's third-grade class is coming in this morning."

After I finish putting out the crayons I ask, "What else can I do?"

Miss Albright looks around. "Well, that's about it, I guess. Thanks for your help."

I go to the table at the back of the room where I always sit when we come to art. It's the table I was sitting at the last time I was in school, the day it happened. I stand here for a minute, wondering what to do. Then I go over to the cabinet where the art supplies are and take out a sketch pad. It's eight-and-a-half by eleven, which is kind of large for me. I am more used to four-by-six pads. This must be one of Miss Albright's.

I find a box of sharpened pencils and sit down at the table. Kids sometimes ask me how I know what to draw. I never know what to say. It's not like I think about anything. I just take a pencil and paper and my hand does the rest. It's like my hands and fingers have brains and eyes.

My hand makes an oval shape and I see Mom's face and quickly I forget where I am. Nothing else matters except making that oval come to life. Mom said once that when you look at a painting of a person, you should be able to feel their heart beating.

I don't know how long I've been working when Miss Albright exclaims, "Oh, my word! Jeremy! It's time for you to go to your room. Hurry. Mrs. Tyler's class will be here in a few minutes."

"Can't I stay in here?" I ask, pleading. "Please. I don't want to go out there and have everybody looking at me. Please, Miss Albright."

She sighs.

"I could help you!" I add.

She smiles. "Well, Mrs. Tyler's class *is* a handful. Let me go talk to Mrs. Worthing and Mr. Zweig."

"Thanks, Miss Albright! Thank you so much!"

A few minutes later she comes back. Mrs. Worthing and Mr. Zweig are with her.

"How are you, Jeremy?" Mrs. Worthing wants to know.

I wish people wouldn't ask me that. What would they do if I said I hurt so much I feel like I want to die? "Okay," I respond, because that's what people want to hear.

"Do you think you could go to your room today?"

"No," I say flatly. "I don't want to see anybody or talk to anybody. I'll be fine in here."

Mrs. Worthing looks at Mr. Zweig. He pulls at the corner of

his mustache. Finally he says, "Well, Jeremy really hasn't missed any assignments." Then he smiles. "To tell the truth, I think he already knows everything I'm going to be teaching for the rest of the year."

I blush and wonder how he knew that. "Except for some things in the back of the math workbook," I say.

"He spends most of his time drawing, anyway. So this is probably the best place for him. Jeremy, you can stop by the room during recess or after school and I'll catch you up on the assignments."

"Would such an arrangement be all right with you, Miss Albright?" Mrs. Worthing wants to know.

"That's fine. And Jeremy would be a great help to me with the younger children."

"Very well," Mrs. Worthing says. "Maybe you'll feel like rejoining your class tomorrow."

"Maybe," I say, because that's what she wants to hear. I'm never going in that room again.

"Thank you, Miss Albright," I say, when Mrs. Worthing and Mr. Zweig leave. "Thank you so much."

She smiles. "You're welcome."

I go back to my picture of Mom. I hear the third graders when their teacher brings them in but really don't pay any attention until I feel somebody next to me and hear a voice say, "What are you doing?"

I turn to see a little girl looking at me very seriously. She has red hair and eyes that are green like summer.

"What are you doing?" she repeats, as if surprised that I haven't answered her.

"What does it look like?"

"No, silly. I mean, what are you doing in this room? You're not in our class. Why aren't you in your room with the kids your age?"

Who is this little girl and why is she asking me these questions like I'm supposed to answer her?

"You draw very well," she continues. "Who is that?"

"My mother."

"She's very pretty. What's your name?"

"Jeremy."

"I'm Sara. Well, since you're here, will you come sit with me and teach me how to draw a turkey? That's what we're supposed to do today."

And before I can answer, she takes my hand. Despite myself I smile and, grasping her hand, follow her to her table near the front of the room.

Jenna

Monday
SCHOOL

Being back is not as bad as I thought it would be. People come up to me at my locker or when they see me in the hall and say they're glad to have me back. People who've never spoken to me and whose names I don't know wave and give me a smile. All of my teachers are understanding, of course, and are ready to cut me as much slack as I want. But I don't want that. I don't want them to do me favors just because of what happened. I mean, don't give me a reason *not* to do any schoolwork. I can do that on my own. But I want to do work now. That's weird, because when Mom was alive I did so little, I was lucky to get Cs.

I am in the cafeteria line. I'm still not that hungry. I don't think I've had a full meal since it happened, and having cold pizza for breakfast doesn't count.

Today is franks-and-beans day. That was always one of my favorites, but I don't want more than a salad. I am just coming out of the cafeteria line and wondering if there's anybody having lunch this period that I would feel comfortable sitting with when I notice a boy walking toward me. He has long blond hair and an earring in his right eyebrow.

"Hi. My name is Gregory. You're Jenna, right?"

He's about my height, maybe a tiny bit taller, and I notice he has a stud in his tongue. He's kind of cute, but what does he want?

"Yes, I'm Jenna."

"Would you sit with me? I have a table over there." He points toward the far end of the cafeteria. Before I can ask him why he thinks I would want to sit with him, he adds, "There's something I'd like to talk with you about."

He's very serious and doesn't have that needy look boys get when they like you. More from curiosity than anything else I say, "Okay."

When we are seated he closes his eyes and bows his head for a minute. Oh, God! He's some religious freak. I'm out of here! I get up from the table.

"Where're you going?" he asks, surprised.

"If you think because my mom is dead that I need God or Jesus or some religious bullshit, you're wrong."

He smiles. "You think because I said grace that I'm some religious nut?"

"Well, aren't you?"

"No. Saying grace was always something my father did. I never did it but since he died, it makes me feel kind of close to him."

He picks up his fork and starts eating his franks and beans. I'm standing here feeling like a fool and he's acting like he doesn't care if I stay or leave, so I sit back down. "Is that why you wanted to talk to me?" I ask.

He eats quietly for a moment, then looks at me. "I remember what it was like the first day I went back to school. Everybody was nice but nobody really knew what I was feeling. I remember wishing I had somebody my own age who knew what it was like."

I nibble at my salad, not daring to look at him. "What do you mean? What was it like for you?"

"It was like I wasn't really inside my body. I could see myself going through the motions and doing all the things that everybody else was doing, but I wasn't there. Sometimes I felt like I was looking down on myself and there was some kind of wall or screen between me and everybody else. I could see them and I knew people's names and I remembered stuff we had done together, but it was like I would never ever feel again what they were feeling and they wouldn't know what I was feeling until one of their parents died, and that might not be for fifty years."

"Yeah. You're right!" I exclaim softly, looking at him. "That's just what it's like. B.T. and A.T. Before Tuesday. After Tuesday. Two different lives almost."

"And you'll never be the person you were before last Tuesday and you have no clue who you are now."

"Yes, yes! That's it! Oh, God! That's really it! It's like my life has stopped, too. Last night I was thinking it was like a freeze-frame in a movie, and I thought this morning the projector would start rolling again. But it didn't and I'm kind of afraid it never will." I look at him intently. "Does it?" I want him to tell me.

He smiles sadly. "I wish I knew. It's been six months since my dad died and nothing has changed that much."

He goes back to eating, but I'm not hungry anymore, not that

I was very hungry to begin with. "Are you new?" I ask him, pushing my tray aside.

"I'm from New York. Outside Albany. I just started school here in September."

"Did your mother decide to move here after your dad died, and what happened to your dad?"

He waits until he finishes eating and takes his tray and mine and puts them on an empty table. "Thanks for asking," he says when he sits down again.

I smile. "You're welcome."

"We're different, Jenna. Even though we look like everybody else when we're changing classes or sitting on the school bus, it's like we live in a different country now. What we want to do almost more than anything is to talk about our parent who died, but people think if they bring it up, we'll start crying or something. But it's just the opposite, you know. When we can talk about them, it makes us feel good and it's like they're still alive, even if it is only inside us."

"Oh, my God. You are so right! Everybody's being real sweet to me today, but nobody has even mentioned my mother. So tell me about your dad."

"It was the second Sunday this past May. He dropped me off for a soccer game at one and said he'd pick me up at four. That was kind of weird because he always stayed for my games, but he said he had something to do. Four o'clock came but my dad wasn't there. The mother of the last kid who got picked up asked me if I needed a ride. I told her yes. My mother was a waitress at a diner and worked second shift so she wasn't around. I was a little worried because this wasn't like my dad.

"When I got home Dad's car was in the driveway. I figured maybe he'd fallen asleep or something. I went in the house and started calling his name. There was no answer. Then I started down to the basement and I smelled this odor like shit. I couldn't imagine what it was. I thought maybe an animal had gotten in the house and died. But when I got down there, my Dad was hanging from a beam."

"Oh, God!"

"Did you know that when somebody gets hung, their bowels let go? That was the shit smell. I ran upstairs and got a knife from the kitchen drawer and cut him down. I didn't know what to do so I just sat there on the basement floor with my father's body lying across my lap. I didn't cry. I didn't do anything. I just sat and looked at my dad. The phone started ringing but I couldn't move. It rang and rang but I couldn't leave my dad by himself. Finally, I heard the door open and my mother calling my name and my dad's. It was she who had been calling, and when nobody answered, she rushed home. I heard her calling for us, but I couldn't answer her. I just waited until she found her way down to the basement and saw us."

"That's awful!"

Gregory nods. "It was pretty bad. I'm not going to lie about that. It was pretty bad."

"Do you know why? Did he leave a note or something?"

"Not that I know of. Maybe he did and my mom never mentioned it. I don't know if she blamed herself or what, but soon after he died, she stopped cooking, cleaning house, or even going to work. All she did was stay in their room with the door closed. I didn't know what to do. Things got so bad that I finally called my grandparents, who live here. They came, took one look, and had her put in a mental hospital and brought me here to live with them."

While he was talking, Gregory's head was down, as if he didn't want me to see his face, but when he finishes, he looks up and his eyes are clear.

"Have you seen your mother?" I ask.

He shakes his head. "I feel kind of guilty, you know, but deep down, I don't want to."

"Why? I mean, how can you not want to see your mother?"

"Because she left me to deal with all this by myself. And my dad! I'm pissed at him, too! He had to know I would be the one to find him."

Gregory is looking at me now as if he's expecting me to say something that will make sense of everything, and I feel bad because I don't know what to say. Did he tell me all this because he thought my mom's being dead and my dad being in jail had given me some kind of magic wand that makes everything better? I know I should say something, but what? What am I supposed to say? I can't handle this. I have to get out of here.

As I get up to go, Gregory says, "I'm sorry. I have had a longer time to think about all this than you have. You're the first person my age I've been able to talk to. I'm sorry for dumping all that on you. You have enough to deal with."

I stop and look at him. I sit back down. "I apologize for getting up like I did just now. Thanks for telling me, for trusting me. It's just that, well, what you went through was so awful."

He looks at me. "No worse than what you went through. Just different. That's all. Just different."

I nod and blink back the tears.

WINTER

Jeremy

MOM'S STUDIO

I think I'll start making the list of Mom's drawings and paintings today. Grandfather Eric said he was going to Manchester to meet with Dad's lawyer. Whatever.

The weekends are hard. If I could sleep late like Mom and Jenna, it would go faster, but I wake up at the same time, even on Saturdays and Sundays. It's like there's a 7:00 A.M. alarm clock inside me. Because it's Saturday I don't have to get up, so I'll lie here for a while and look out the window at the branches of the birch tree and the sky. I'm seeing what Mom saw when she woke up every day. I have to see for both of us now.

This morning the sky is white like birch bark. It's the kind of sky Mom would look at and say, "Looks like snow, Jeremy." And it would always snow! That's about all it's done since right before Christmas. I've never seen so much snow. Grandfather Eric keeps a path shoveled so I can get from here to the house and back, even though he keeps grumbling about how much easier it would be if I slept in the house. But I don't miss Mom as much out here.

I wish she could see the snow. It's piled so high it's like walking through a tunnel.

I don't like Mom being dead. I'm not used to having to think about what to do with my time. When Mom was here, time didn't matter. I was happy just being in the same room where she was. She didn't have to talk to me and I didn't have to be doing anything. I liked to sit in the kitchen while she cooked. Sometimes she'd give me a job, like sorting dried beans and taking out the bad ones and the stones, or separating the little white things out of crushed red pepper. When she was working here in the studio, I would lie on the couch downstairs and look through her art books. Sometimes she'd ask me to wash out a brush or bring up some clean rags from the plastic bag she kept beneath the sink.

Everything was easier when Mom was around. Now I have to think about so much stuff. Every day when school's out I have to decide whether to go home with Sara or Miss Albright. I used to go to Miss Albright's almost every day. I like it at her house. She has prints of famous paintings and posters from museums on the walls. But her house is small, I guess because she's not married and doesn't have any kids. There're only two bedrooms, and she uses the spare one for her studio. I have to sleep on the couch in the living room.

Sara's house is bigger. Her dad owns a computer store and there're computers in almost every room! Since coming back after Christmas vacation, I sleep at Sara's almost every night. I have a room all my own right next to hers. Any other Saturday I would go over there, but Bob and Elaine, Sara's parents, are going to Montreal to visit Bob's brother. He's not Bob's real brother. Sara said he was adopted.

Sunday nights I always go to Karen's for pizza, and stay over. Since Jenna and I don't live in the same house anymore, Karen thought it would be good if Jenna and I saw each other once a week. But Jenna's going out with this Gregory guy, so she's usually at his house. Even when I do see her we don't talk. Not since what happened at Thanksgiving.

Thanksgiving dinner was at Karen's. It was just me, Jenna, Miss Albright, and Grandfather Eric. That Gregory guy had to spend Thanksgiving with his grandparents and Jenna let us all know *several* times that that's where *she* wished *she* was and that's where *she* was going at seven o'clock so could we just *please* hurry up with dinner. She could've left right then for all I cared.

It was only a couple of weeks after it happened, and I know I was kind of depressed. I think that's the word. It was like I was stuck in mud up to my neck, and it was hard to move and hard to cry out for help. I was trying to remember what last Thanksgiving was like and couldn't. Why couldn't I remember anything about the last Thanksgiving with Mom? I wanted to ask Jenna if she remembered anything, but I didn't want to take the chance of her saying something mean to me. Karen had been there, like always, and I could've asked her, but she and Grandfather Eric were talking about Grandmother Dorothy and different people back in Pennsylvania, and a lot of them had died, too. Because Karen and my dad used to be married, she and Grandfather Eric have known each other a long time. I felt kind of sorry for him. It seems like most everybody he knew is dead.

Every Thanksgiving when it was time to eat, Dad would ask us to say what we were thankful for. I was afraid Karen was going to ask us this year, but she didn't. I would've said, "Nothing." We had just started to chow down real good when Grandfather Eric told Karen that Dad was always asking about her and wondered why she never came to visit him. Karen said she didn't think Thanksgiving dinner was the right time to talk about it. For some reason, that made Grandfather Eric angry. But he's always angry these days. All he does is talk on the phone with Dad's lawyer or read books about something called an insanity defense. The table in the family room is piled high with legal books and magazines. He calls them *journals*. Whatever. He says Dad was crazy when he did it, but he's all right now. Doesn't make sense to me. Either you're crazy or you're not.

Anyway, when Karen said she didn't want to talk about it, Grandfather Eric started yelling about how he had always thought Karen was a cold bitch who had about as much feeling as a turkey bone because she didn't give a damn that Dad was sitting in jail on Thanksgiving so depressed that he wanted to kill himself. That's when I said, "If he hadn't killed Mom, he wouldn't be in jail." The words just came out without me even thinking about them. But I didn't like him yelling at Karen and calling her a name. Next thing I knew, Grandfather Eric was yelling at me and saying I wasn't much of a son because I hadn't been to see Dad, either. At least Jenna sent a drawing, he said, but I hadn't even done that!

I don't know what happened but I lost it. It was like something inside me cracked open and all these tears and sobs came pouring out and I couldn't stop them. One minute I had been looking at Grandfather Eric yelling at Karen and turning red in the face and spit was flying out of his mouth, and the next thing I knew spit and red were flying at me and I freaked. I was crying so hard my chest started hurting and I was having a hard time catching my breath and I don't know. Maybe I was afraid I was dying, because I was having a hard time breathing and I fell on the floor and started kicking and screaming and flinging my arms around. Man, I've never done anything like that in my life!

I'm glad Miss Albright was there. She threw herself on top of me and pinned my my arms and legs to the floor so I would stop kicking and flailing around, and kept whispering in my ear, "Shh. It's all right, Jeremy. Shh." It took a couple of minutes before I could catch my breath and stop crying, but even then I was still breathing hard and making little whimpering sounds.

That was about the time Jenna said, "Fuck this! I can't stay here a minute longer! It would've been better if we'd gone to McDonald's or Pizza Hut for Thanksgiving instead of trying to pretend that we're normal. Rachel's in the cemetery and Dad's in jail! How fucking normal is that? Thanks, God! Thanks a fucking lot! Will somebody please take me to Gregory's. Please! I have *got* to get out of here or I'll *scream!*"

I started crying again and Karen helped Miss Albright take me into the living room. She sat down on the couch and rocked me in her arms like I was a little baby. I don't remember falling asleep but I did, because when I woke up there was a blanket over me and the room was dark except for the soft light from the lamp at the end of the couch, where Miss Albright was sitting, reading a book. The house was real quiet and I closed my eyes again and just lay there a while listening to the stillness.

Eventually I opened my eyes and asked Miss Albright where everybody was. She said Karen was upstairs and that Grandfather Eric had taken Jenna to that Gregory guy's house and then gone home. She said he said to tell me he was real sorry for yelling at me and for what he said. He told me the same thing when I got home the next day.

I hear the garage door going up, the sound of a car door closing, and the car backing out of the garage. Now the garage door is going down, the car door shuts again, and the car backs out of the driveway. The sound of the car is quieter and quieter as it goes up the street and then it is silent again.

He's gone and I'm glad. I used to like going to his house. It's so big and there's a meadow and fields and a pond and all kinds of trees, and we used to go for walks, him and me and Mom, and he'd show us all kinds of neat stuff, like holes where foxes and groundhogs lived and trees that beavers were cutting down with their teeth! I thought him living here with me would be good. He would show me stuff in the field back of our house like he used to before Grandmother Dorothy died. I thought, too, that if he was still sad because Grandmother Dorothy died, then he would understand how I was feeling and I would understand how he was feeling and that would cheer both of us up. But that's not how it's been.

I go downstairs, wash up, and get dressed. Even though it's not far from here to the house, I put on my hooded jacket, lock the studio door behind me, and hurry into the house. Grandfather Eric said when it's this cold and the wind's blowing, my skin could freeze in a couple of seconds.

I take some waffles and sausages out of the refrigerator-freezer and put the waffles in the toaster and the sausage on a dish and stick it in the microwave. It's still weird being in the house and neither Mom nor Dad being here. Right after it happened, I could see Mom all the time—sitting at the kitchen table, walking across the yard from the studio, cooking at the stove, sitting at her drawing board. So I started drawing her—her face, her sitting on the butcher-block couch in front of the fireplace, her upstairs in the studio staring out the window, her taking a nap.

One day close to Christmas vacation time, Sara's class came to the art room to draw Santa Clauses. Sara came back to where I was in the back drawing pictures of Mom.

"How many pictures of your mom are you going to draw?" I told her my mom is dead, but that's all. I looked at her and shrugged.

"I don't understand why you're always drawing pictures of your mother," she went on, "when you could be drawing pictures of me and showing me how to draw Santa." So I turned the page and did a quick sketch of her sitting on Santa's lap. When she showed it to the other kids, they wanted me to draw pictures of them on Santa's lap. Before I knew it, a whole morning had gone by and I hadn't thought about Mom. I felt really awful. I was afraid if I didn't think about her all the time, then she really would be dead.

Everybody had gone to lunch and only me and Miss Albright were in the room and I started crying because I had been having a good time and forgotten about Mom, but Miss Albright told me it was okay. She said Mom wouldn't want me to spend all my time thinking about her, that Mom would want me to do stuff and be happy and that even though my mind might not think about her all the time, my heart would never forget her. And that made sense.

I used to visit Mom every morning on my way to school, until it got real cold and started snowing a lot. I liked standing at her grave. It reminded me of when she took naps on Saturday and Sunday afternoons. The whole time she was asleep, it was like I had her to myself. That's how it was standing at her grave. I hope she's not too lonely because I can't visit now.

I finish eating and put my plate and silverware in the dishwasher. It's time to get to work. Mom called it making an inventory. She and I started working on one this past summer. She would have me write down the name of the painting or drawing, the size, and a short description of what it looked like, if there wasn't a title on the back. Bob said I could borrow a laptop computer, but I think I want to write everything down first. Then I'll put it on the computer.

It's still hard for me to believe that Mom put in her will that I could have the studio and all her paintings and drawings. Karen took us to see Mom's lawyer, some woman with silvery hair and a mole at the corner of her mouth, but she's not old like Gran, who also has silvery hair. I didn't know Mom had a lawyer or a will. The lawyer said Mom had changed it a couple of weeks before everything happened. Maybe she had a feeling.

The lawyer read the will, but I didn't understand a word until she stopped reading and explained that Mom had given everything to me and Jenna. Mom and Dad owned the house, the studio, and the field together, so Mom willed her half of the house to Jenna. I wondered which half that was, but the lawyer said it wasn't like that. I didn't know what she meant but decided to drop it. Mom gave the studio and all her paintings and drawings to me. She had a lot of money in the bank from people and museums buying her paintings and from investments, and all that was split half-and-half between me and Jenna. But we can't go to the bank and get the money until we're twenty-two. In the meantime, the money is to be used to take care of us and for college. Mom also said in her will that if anything happened to her and Dad, she wanted Karen to be our guardian.

We were hardly out of the lawyer's office before Jenna started cursing Mom. Except she called her Rachel. Jenna thought Mom had given me more than her, and she didn't believe it when Karen said that wasn't true. Jenna said the paintings were worth a lot of money and she should have been given some of them.

"Well, you're just going to have to sell them and give the money to Dad to help pay for his defense," Jenna said to me, as we got in the car.

"Why don't you and Dad sell the house?" I shot back.

"How can we sell the house, stupid, when you own the studio?"

"Tough titty," I told her.

"I hate you!" she screamed, jumped out of the car and slammed the door. Karen sat there real quiet for a minute. Mom would have gone after Jenna, but Karen didn't. She just sat and finally turned the key, started the car, and drove off.

I don't know why, but I miss Jenna. When we went to California over Christmas vacation I was sure she would talk and joke with me and things would be like always, but all the way there and all the way back she either had her headphones on listening to a CD, or her nose stuck in some fashion magazine, or was asleep, or pretending to be.

Being in California was okay. I stayed in Mom's room. Even though it rained a lot, I started thinking that it might not be too bad to live there. It was nice being around Gran and Grampy, because they miss Mom, too. They might miss her even more than I do, because they knew her longer. I liked hearing them tell stories about when she was a little girl and showing me pictures of her from when she was born until she graduated college. They also have a lot of Mom's drawings from when she was a little girl until she married Dad, and for a Christmas present they gave me and Jen a photo album with copies of all the photos they had of Mom. Jenna also got to go shopping with Gran. Grampy took me to a museum and bought me the book of paintings by Georgia O'Keeffe, the one I'd wanted to give Mom.

I go back to the studio and lock the door behind me. I keep the studio locked whether I'm in it or not. The only person who can come in here is Miss Albright. I have Mom's cell phone so I can call somebody if I need to.

It's hard to know where to start. Mom has canvases stacked up all along one wall, and then there are sketch pads and drawings in the file. This is going to be hard because I don't know which ones she thought were good and which ones she didn't. But Bob said people will be interested in everything Mom did.

I slide open the top drawer of the file, curious about what's in it. I would see Mom putting drawings in here, but I never saw what they were. The file cabinet is long and flat, with wide, thin drawers. Each drawer is crammed with sketchbooks and sheets of paper on which Mom sketched out ideas.

At the back of the bottom drawer I see a book. The cover is a nice photograph of purple flowers. I open it. It's filled with Mom's handwriting. It's her diary! I didn't know Mom had a diary! I hold it in my hand, wondering if it would be okay for me to read it. What if there's something in it about me? Like maybe Mom didn't like me or something. No. That's stupid. Or maybe I was adopted. Or maybe Mom wrote in it that she was fooling around like Dad said. But I just know she wouldn't do something like that. I just know it!

JUNE 8

How did I become a stranger in my own house? We used to eat dinner together, all four of us, but in the past few weeks, Eric and Jenna always have something more important to do—watch a TV show or she needs to go to the mall and he has to take her, or there's some "cool" new song that she just <u>has</u> to play for him on the CD player up in her room. When I say I would like to hear it, she says, "Oh, Mom. You wouldn't like it." "How would I know if I don't hear it?" I answer back. "Trust me," she says over her shoulder as she's leaving the room. And Eric follows her up the stairs, a self-satisfied smirk on his face.

But he stole her from me when she was still a baby, by giving her expensive gifts for her birthday and Christmas. I would tell him I thought he was trying to buy her. He said I was getting upset about nothing. But I knew otherwise. I kept at it and finally I thought I'd convinced him that we would buy presents together and everything would be from both of us. So for her next birthday, Eric and I agreed that our present would be a Raggedy Ann doll. Imagine my surprise when Eric gives her Barbie with a complete wardrobe! What was I supposed to do? Start competing with him to see who could buy her the most expensive presents, or take his expensive gifts away from her, or do nothing? I did nothing.

I never cared that Dad always gave Jenna better things than me. Maybe if I had wanted the stuff it would've been different, but I was more like Mom and I didn't care about clothes and stuff like that. And, anyway, Mom gave me really good presents, like my computer and art books. Dad would get me video games but never any of the really cool ones. It was like he knew everything that Jenna liked and Mom knew everything I liked. But Jenna was Dad's favorite and I was Mom's and Jenna and I knew and it was okay. I guess Mom didn't know that it was okay with us.

JUNE 23

I tried to talk to Eric about the way he and Jenna act with each other. I don't like it when he and Jenna stop laughing and talking when I come in the room and start up again the instant I leave. I don't like it when the two of them give each other looks across the table at Sunday brunch and start giggling. He says it's father-daughter bonding, that it's important for them to have a close relationship because it means she'll have healthy relationships with boys. That sounds good, but I don't understand why I have to feel like an outsider in my own daughter's life.

I wonder if things would be different if Eric and I were closer. I was reading an article in a magazine at the dentist's about how to save your marriage. It said that if you started remembering what brought the two of you together and started to relive the memories of when you first fell in love, you would fall in love all over again. That won't work for me.

When I think about the beginning of my relationship with Eric, I feel ashamed. I've always felt ashamed. I remember the day we went to get our marriage license at the town hall. Every week the Birchfield newspaper prints the names of people who took out marriage licenses the week before. When we went to get ours I asked the clerk if our names had to be in the paper. She said no and I told her not to put ours in. Eric thought it was because I like privacy. How could he be so dense and still be a therapist? What woman doesn't want the whole world to know that she's getting married? The fact that I didn't want it in the paper, that I didn't invite anyone to our wedding, that we had a justice of the peace do the ceremony, that I didn't even tell my parents until afterward should have made him wonder.

I had tried to talk to him about it, but he didn't see anything wrong with him having been my therapist. He said therapy was the only place two people could really get to know each other. It took me a long while before I figured out that the only one getting to know anybody was him getting to know me.

I thought about Sandra Callahan the other day for the first time in years. She had an affair with our high school English teacher, Mr. Davis. She was sixteen. They got married and that saved his job. This was before we knew a lot about sexual harassment. Now he'd probably be arrested. A couple of years later, when I was home for the summer from college, I happened to run into her waiting for the bus near Union Square. She was very pregnant and it was obvious to me that she wasn't happy, so I asked if she wanted to go for coffee. We did and when I asked how things were going, she said she liked Arthur—Mr. Davis—better as her English teacher. He had read poetry to her then, but when he became her husband the poetry stopped.

Eric and I hadn't been married long when one day I told him, "I liked you better when you were my therapist. I feel like I got the best part of you then." I honestly thought he would respond to me the way he had when he was my therapist and say he wanted to hear more about what I was feeling. That was why I fell in love with him. He was the first person who ever cared about my feelings. How could I not have wanted to marry him? But he was furious and started yelling that I wasn't being realistic. How could I expect him to devote as much time to my feelings now as he had when he was my therapist? Nobody could be that patient and that good a listener in real life, he said in this tone of voice as if I was the stupidest person he'd ever met.

I wish he'd told me when I was still his patient. I didn't understand how he could care so much about my feelings when I was paying him and not care after he married me. I had thought I was marrying a man who had helped me learn to express my feelings. But I ended up with one who got angry when I did. It was like he was two different people.

If you can't tell your husband how you feel, it's not a marriage.

JULY 15

I have moved into the studio. I told him I have some projects to do and that I need a lot of time and space to get them done. I guess I was hoping he would say something more than okay, but he didn't.

The only one who's upset is Jeremy. He wants to move to the studio with me. The anguish on his face tells me what I don't want to admit. Eric and I are separating and the children have already chosen sides.

I don't want to read any more right now. It's weird reading what Mom was thinking and feeling. I wish Jenna was here. She would probably understand a lot more and could explain it to me. But I understood one thing. I didn't know Dad had been Mom's therapist. He and Mom always told us they met at an art show on campus.

I remember the day Mom moved into the studio. It was a Saturday morning. I was sitting on the deck. It was hot and I was thinking about riding my bike over to the pool at the high school when I saw her come out the back door and go toward the studio, carrying a box. I ran to hold the studio door open for her.

"What're you doing?" I asked.

"I've got a lot of work to do so I'm going to be living in the studio for a while."

"How long?" I asked. My voice started trembling and I was

afraid I was going to cry because I didn't want to be in the house with just Dad and Jenna.

She told me not to worry. "I'll be right here whenever you need me."

And I said, "But I want you around even when I don't need you."

I thought I saw her eyes tear up, but I'm not sure. Then I asked if she and Dad were going to get a divorce. She smiled and said, "Of course not, sweetheart."

I knew she was trying to make me feel better, but she didn't.

I look out the window. It is starting to snow.

Jenna

THE JAIL

Since Christmas vacation I've been going with Grandfather Eric every Wednesday to visit Dad. But today as I walk out of school, I hope his car won't be in the parking lot. But it is.

"My grandfather's here," I say to Gregory, who is walking next to me.

"Call me when you get back?"

"Don't I always?"

He goes to give me a kiss and I push him away. Before I can stop him he grabs at my breasts through my jacket. With this heavy jacket and sweater on, he knows he won't feel anything, but that's not the point. He's always trying to put his hands on me or kiss me when we're out in public. He does it to show off, like I'm some prize he won, and it's really starting to piss me off.

Gregory likes me to wait until he gets a seat on the school bus so he can blow me a kiss through the window, but the wind's blowing and I'm freezing. I hurry between two buses, across the driveway, and to the parking lot.

"Hi." I greet Grandfather Eric, my voice flat.

"Afternoon," he says, turning the key in the ignition. I've hardly gotten my seat belt fastened before he drives away. He never asks me how I am or anything about school. All he thinks about is the trial and getting Dad out of jail. Karen reminds me that Dad is all he has left since Grandmother Dorothy died, and I feel for him, I really do, but none of this is easy for me, either. I think about Dad getting out of jail, but then I try to imagine living at home with him again and I get scared.

When I came back after Christmas vacation, it seemed like a good idea to start going to see him once a week. I had sent him the drawing and he wrote back and thanked me, but I didn't answer. It was just too much to deal with. Gregory kept saying I couldn't spend the rest of my life avoiding him. I told him to take his own advice and go see his mother.

I'd been wanting to see Dad but could never figure out what we would talk about. I was also scared of what Karen would think if I went to see him. Anytime I brought him up she didn't say much, and I got the feeling that she's not on Dad's side but didn't say anything because she didn't want to hurt my feelings. I can respect that. But I didn't want to have to lie and sneak to go see my own father, so when I came back from California I told her I was thinking about doing it. I was surprised when she said she thought it was a good idea. When I asked her why, she said, "Because he's your father."

The first time Grandfather Eric took me, I got in his car and, without thinking, turned on the car radio and started scanning the stations. That's what I always did whenever I went anywhere with Mom or Dad.

"Turn that thing off," Grandfather Eric snapped. The next week I brought my CD player and headphones, but he said he could hear it anyway. So there's nothing to do but sit here and think, which is something I try real hard not to do.

I do my best to keep my mind occupied as much as possible, which is why I made straight As last term. Me. Jenna. Straight As! It's like Gregory says: Things change when something happens to your parents. You either fall apart or you get your shit together. I've never studied so much in my life.

Gregory gets annoyed with me because it seems like that's all I want to do. Which isn't true. It's just that he and I can't seem to agree on anything anymore, not even what movies to see. He left me in the theater when we went to see *Titanic,* and after a half hour of *Starship Troopers,* I was out of there! I had better things to do with my life than spend time watching white people kill giant bugs. I went to Bloomie's and hung out at the makeup counter, where I started telling customers what color lipstick they should use, and after watching me in action for a little while, the lady at the makeup counter offered me a job and almost fainted when I told her I was fourteen. When Gregory and I hooked up again after *Starship Troopers* and I told him what I'd been doing, he said I was pretty enough without makeup and why couldn't women be content with natural beauty and stuff like that. I asked him where he got the idea that nature was perfect. Nature can always stand some improving on. And we spent the rest of the time arguing. Lately I can't say anything without him picking a fight. We're either fighting over really stupid stuff or I'm pushing his hands away from where they don't belong.

When I was in California over Christmas, I was surprised that I didn't miss him as much as I thought I was going to. Having a boyfriend is nice, but it can get tired pretty quick—having somebody who wants to be with you all the time, who wants to know what you've been doing and what you've been thinking. So after I got back I didn't call him right away. I should have, but I knew that once I did, he'd want to see me and if I saw him he'd want to feel me up. He said I'm a tease. Bullshit! I told him just because I wear something so he can see some cleavage, it's not an invitation to touch. It's an invitation to look and that's all! But I guess guys can't look and not want to touch. I like Gregory. I don't think I could have held it together as well as I have if he hadn't come along. But I feel like he's made me the center of his life and I don't want to be and I think he's hurt because he's not the center of my life. But I don't want a center. Mom made painting the center of her life and I hated it. When you have a center you hurt people, so I'm not going to have one.

Exit Ten. Five miles. Every week when I see the sign it feels like some kind of death sentence. It's where we get off. Ten more minutes and we'll be at the jail. That place gives me the creeps worse than a funeral home, because the people in jail aren't dead but they might as well be. And that includes Dad. That first time I went he didn't know I was coming, and when he came into the visitors room he stopped when he saw me. Maybe it was because of the look on my face. The last time I had seen him he was this tall guy with thick dark hair that he was always pushing back off his forehead who wore rimless glasses that didn't hide his beautiful blue eyes. He always had on his preppy uniform—khaki pants, a Brooks Brothers shirt, cashmere sweater, and loafers—and when he smiled, there was a boyishness about him that made you want to put your arms around him.

The man I saw that day was skinny. He had short hair that looked like it had been cut with a pair of dull scissors by someone who had just wanted to get the job over with. The glasses were the same, but the eyes behind them were not. Dad's eyes were always filled with love and mischief. This man's eyes were full of fear and hurt. They had taken my dad away and replaced him with a scared man wearing an ill-fitting orange jumpsuit. Dad could probably see in my face that I was sorry I had come, and I was.

But when Dad's face broke into a huge grin, he looked more like the dad I remembered, and he hurried over and gave me a big hug. It had been so long since I had felt his arms around me, and I wanted his hug to make me feel safe like it always had. But it didn't.

There's a table and a couch in the visitors room, and Dad and I sat down across from each other while Grandfather Eric sat on the couch. Dad and I just kind of sat there, neither one of us knowing how to act or what to say. I don't know what I expected. Maybe that he would tell me he didn't do it, that he was being framed like in the movies. But he didn't.

"How're you doing?" I asked him, knowing it was a stupid thing to ask somebody who was locked up in jail, but I didn't know what else to say.

"Okay," he said, but I could tell that he wasn't okay.

I started to feel sorry for him, and then remembered and got confused.

"How's school?"

"Okay. I got all As last term."

"That's great!" he exclaimed, but in that fake voice adults use when they're trying to care about what you're telling them but they really don't.

He wanted to know what movies I'd seen recently and what were the hot new CDs, and I know he was trying to make things seem like they were normal, but how could we talk as if nothing had happened? It wasn't normal to be talking with your father in jail, even if they had tried to make the visitors room look family-like. But with an armed guard standing right outside the door and windows all around for anybody walking by to look through, it was hard to act normal.

After the most awkward ten minutes of my life, Dad said he was glad to see me but he and Grandfather Eric had to talk about the trial, which starts in June, so I went and sat on the couch and Grandfather Eric went and sat at the table. I heard Grandfather Eric say he had hired a private detective to find the man Rachel was having an affair with. If they can find him and get him to testify, then a jury might say it was justifiable homicide. A man shoots a woman because she's screwing around and it's okay for him to kill her? That's bullshit!

When it was time to go, Dad gave me another hug, but I didn't feel anything. I still don't. Maybe I keep going because I hope the hugs will start to feel like they used to and Dad will tell me what happened. Maybe if he told me why he did it. I know what he said in his letter, but that doesn't make sense. So what if Rachel was seeing somebody else? Everybody screws around and it's no big deal. And anyway, Dad's a therapist. He's supposed to know how to talk about things like that. He was always asking us about our feelings. But it just occurred to me: I don't think he ever told us how he felt about anything.

The jail sits to itself on a hill off Route Ten. But the first thing I always notice are the fences. There are three of them, high fences made of wire, and on top of each one are rolls of wire that look like they're made of razor blades.

There's an American and a state flag on a pole right outside the jail, and they're standing straight out in the wind. It reminds me of when I was around six or seven; almost every Sunday afternoon in the spring, Mom and Dad would take me and Jeremy to the bluff at the edge of the campus to fly kites. It seemed like the wind knew there were kites to play with, because all you had to do was let out your string and the wind rose up the side of the hill and almost snatched the kite out of your hands. It was all you could do to let the string out fast enough. I remember Mom's cheek next to mine and her hands holding mine as mine held the kite string, and that reminds me of when she used to read to me at night. Even after Jeremy was born and was old enough to be read to, she still read to me first because I was the oldest. And then when I was eleven, I told her I didn't want her reading to me anymore like I was a baby. But for a long time after that, I would press my ear against the wall and try to listen as she read to Jeremy in his room next door.

Why do things change? I don't want to be six or eleven again, but I wish the feeling of Mom's cheek next to mine or her sitting on the edge of my bed reading to me hadn't gone away. What happened? How did my mother end up dead and my dad in jail? You get up one morning and go to school like you've done almost every morning of your life and it's a day like all the other days until the principal pulls you out of class and you find out that your dad killed your mom.

That's nuts! I mean, I know it happens, but not to me. That kind of stuff happens in homes like you see on the news, where the fathers beat their wives and children, are alcoholic, or lost their jobs or something. But Mom and Dad weren't fighting and Dad didn't drink and he had a good job. So what if Mom was living in the studio and she and Dad didn't talk much? Big deal. Most of my friends' parents don't talk to each other, either. As far as I can tell, that's what it's like to be married.

Grandfather Eric finds a spot in the parking lot. We hurry inside and sign the visitors book. A guard runs a metal detector over our bodies and then takes us to the visitors room.

We've only been there a few minutes when Dad is brought in, looking as bad this week as he has all the others I've been here. Maybe a little worse because he doesn't look like he's combed his hair or shaved for a couple of days. We hug but there's no enthusiasm in it for either of us.

We sit down at the table and I wait for Dad to ask me the usual boring questions about school but he fools me.

"Sweetheart, there's something I need to talk to you about."

"Sure. What, Dad?" I respond more casually than I'm feeling.

"You remember how Rachel and I used to fight a lot?"

I look at him curiously. "No. Not really. I mean, I remember that time she slapped you because you took me to get my piercings."

"Yes! That's what I mean!" he says, almost too excited. "And what about the other times?"

"I—I don't remember any other times. You guys never fought. Maybe you should have."

Dad smiles, but it's not one that makes me want to smile back. "Maybe *fought* is too strong a word. You do remember the times she yelled at me about something."

I nod reluctantly. "Sure, but she yelled at me more than she did you."

"That's what I mean!" Dad responds, getting excited again. "She did yell at you a lot. Sweetheart, I'm not asking you to remember things that didn't happen. But I might need you to testify at the trial about her slapping me and yelling at me and at you. It would really help me a lot. All you would have to do would be to tell the jury what you saw and heard. To tell the truth. That's all."

I don't know what to say.

"Please think about it. And talk to your brother, too. My lawyer believes it would really help my case a lot if you and Jeremy testified on my behalf. We can talk more about it next week if you want."

If he thinks Jeremy will testify for him, he's really lost it. He has turned away and Grandfather Eric, who has been sitting on the couch, comes over to the table. I go sit on the couch. I wish I knew how to drive. I need to get out of here. Now!

Jeremy

Grandfather Eric called a little while ago and asked me to come to the house. I wondered what he wanted. He's not supposed to try and make me go see Dad like he was doing, telling me how Jenna went once a week. Jenna's a jerk! I asked Karen if I had to go and she said I didn't and what she says counts because she's our legal guardian now, which means that she has Mom's power even if she's not my mom, and she told Grandfather Eric to stop trying to make me go see Dad. So I didn't know why Grandfather Eric wanted me to come to the house. When I got here I found out it was to meet Dad's lawyer.

He gave me that fake smile adults put on when they aren't used to being around children and they're trying to make us believe that we're going to have fun with them. Yeah, right! Then I thought about Sara and didn't smile back. I wonder how she got to be the way she is. She's only eight, but she's so sure about what she wants and doesn't want, what she likes and doesn't like. The first day we met it was like she had already decided I was going to be her friend. School was letting out and I was going to stay in Miss Albright's room until all the kids had left and then go to the studio. But Sara walked in the room, came over to me, and said, "Are you ready to go, Jeremy?" I had no idea what she meant, but she took my hand, told me to get my coat and that I was going home on the bus with her. And I did.

One day some kids on the bus started teasing me about being her boyfriend. Sara told them I was her brother, like Francis, her father's adopted brother. Later I tried to explain to her that I really wasn't her brother, and she said I felt like her brother so that meant I was just like her father and Francis.

I like being with her. We play with her dolls, make popcorn in the fireplace, watch TV, and draw. She's not very good but that's okay. She'll take crayons and fill a page with different colors of scribbles, and then we'll take turns trying to decide what it looks like. We giggle a lot, too.

Her parents are nice. Bob and Elaine. Elaine has red hair and green eyes like Sara. When I'm at their house what happened seems far away. Sometimes it's almost like it happened to somebody else. What's really weird, though, is that if nothing had happened, I wouldn't know Sara.

The lawyer and Grandfather Eric have been talking to me about Dad and what a great man he is and what a wonderful contribution he can still make to society and how a man like my dad shouldn't be locked up in prison for the rest of his life when he can still contribute so much to society. "But I don't know if any of that can happen if we don't get your cooperation, Jeremy," the lawyer says, giving me a serious look.

We are sitting in the living room. I am on the couch, and Grandfather Eric and the lawyer have pulled up the two leather chairs and are facing me.

"I need to ask you some questions, if you don't mind." The lawyer smiles like he's my friend, but he didn't even tell me his name.

I think for a minute. Then I tell him, "I mind, but you can ask."

The lawyer looks surprised. Then he smiles. "Thank you for being honest. I hope you'll be just as honest in answering my questions. Did your mother and father ever argue with each other?"

I wonder why he wants to know that. Then it occurs to me. It's like the trials I see on Court TV. If somebody has a good enough reason for doing something, then it's like it was okay that they did it. So if I say Mom and Dad argued a lot, then it'll be okay that Dad killed her. "No sir."

"They didn't? Your sister says your mother got angry all the time."

I hate Jenna! I just look at the lawyer.

"What do you have to say to that?" the lawyer asks.

"Nothing. My sister and I don't talk much. And anyway, she'll say anything. You don't know her like I do."

Grandfather Eric frowns at me and opens his mouth as if he's going to say something, but the lawyer holds up his hand and Grandfather Eric closes his mouth. "Did you ever see your mother strike your father?" the lawyer wants to know.

She smacked Dad really hard that day Jenna came back with her navel pierced. "No sir."

The lawyer leans forward. "Do you know what a lie is, Jeremy?"

"Sure."

"Then why are you telling one? Are you afraid to tell me the truth because you think you'll be betraying your mother? Well, I'm sorry about what happened to your mother, Jeremy. I really am. But as hard as it may be to get used to, she's not with us anymore. Your father is. When your dad's trial starts, it would mean a lot for his case if you would say in court what you know about the arguments between your parents, and especially the morning she slapped him because he took your sister to get some body piercings."

"I don't remember that," I say. *And anyway, it didn't happen in the morning. It was in the evening, and if you don't know that, you're not much of a lawyer.*

"You don't remember or you don't want to say?" The lawyer has raised his voice and is looking at me with eyes as hard as ice. I don't like him and I don't want to listen to him anymore.

"All I remember is that Dad killed my mom." I say it quietly but firmly, like Sara. Then I get up and run out of the room.

"Jeremy! We're not finished!" Grandfather Eric calls after me, but I'm out the door and rush back to the studio and lock the door. I take Mom's diary out of the bottom drawer of the file. That's where I put the card Grampy gave me at Christmas with his phone number on it. He used to be a lawyer, but he's retired now.

"Hello." I hear Grampy's voice. I'm glad he picked up and not Gran.

"Grampy. It's Jeremy."

"Jeremy! My, my! I don't believe you've ever called us. Is everything all right?"

"I guess. Well, I don't know. I mean, I'm not sure."

"What's the matter, son?"

"Can they make me say things at Dad's trial?"

"Does somebody want you to testify at the trial? Who? Eric's lawyer?" He sounds like he's getting upset, even angry.

"Yes. He just asked me a lot of questions about Mom and Dad having arguments and whether they ever had fights."

"What did you tell him?"

"That I didn't remember."

Grampy chuckles. "Good for you, son. You just keep saying that and you won't have to take the stand when Eric goes on trial. They can't make you."

"But—but what if I do remember?"

"That doesn't mean you have to tell, does it?"

"No. No, it doesn't."

"Don't worry, Jeremy. Helen and I will be there when the trial starts. We'll protect you."

I feel better now. "Thanks, Grampy. Tell Gran I said hello."

"I'll do that."

"Bye."

"Good-bye."

When the lawyer was talking to me, it was like Mom wasn't important anymore, like she didn't even exist. The lawyer talked like it didn't matter what happened. He didn't even care that Mom's dead. Well, it wasn't his mother. And so what if Mom slapped Dad? He didn't have to do what he did, no matter what the lawyer thinks.

AUGUST 21

Eric and Jenna barely speak to me since I slapped him. I couldn't believe he let that child get her navel and nipple pierced. What got into him? Why can't he say no to her? I wanted to slap her, but knew I would regret it for the rest of my life.

Maybe it's all my fault. I'm the one who moved out of the house and left her to him. Maybe I should have slapped him when he had the nerve to tell her that I didn't want her to have the Barbie doll but he thought she was old enough. What girl can resist a father who buys her expensive gifts and treats her like his girlfriend? And why wouldn't she hate the mother who tried to come between them? So what if she hated me? No. No. I don't want my daughter to hate me like I hate my mother. But I remember something Mother told me once. It didn't make sense at the time. She had seen an interview on television with the actress Bette Davis, who said that if your children don't hate you some of the time, then you aren't much of a parent. When Mother told me that, I was outraged and swore I would never be that kind of a mother. But if saving Jenna means that she will hate me, what's more important? My feelings or my daughter's well-being?

God, I feel like such a coward!

AUGUST 25

If he's sleeping with her I'll kill him! It's hard for me to believe Eric would do that. But isn't that what every mother says when she finds out her husband has been sleeping with her daughter?

She was lying on the deck this afternoon sinbathing—isn't that an interesting slip of the pen—I mean sunbathing, in a bikini which left nothing to the imagination. Eric was sitting in a beach chair wearing a pair of shorts and no shirt. Jenna's head was next to his bare feet. He was looking at some journal that was in his lap, but I couldn't tell if his eyes were on it or Jenna's breasts. Then I noticed the bottle of suntan oil on the floor next to him.

I was going to go in the house to take some hamburger out of the freezer for dinner, but I never made it. I walked across the lawn and onto the deck, and maybe if she had opened her eyes to see who it was or given me some kind of recognition, I wouldn't have gotten so angry. But she was lying there on her back, body glistening with suntan lotion, eyes closed, and a little smirk on her face like she knew it was me staring down at her and she could care less.

I told her I didn't want her lying around half naked in front of her father and that I was glad Jeremy had gone swimming because I sure didn't want her flaunting her body around him.

"What's with you?" she shot back. "If we were at the beach, you wouldn't have said a word."

"But we're not at the beach," I returned, weakly, angry at myself for not being able to think of something that would have shut her up.

"But what's the difference? All I'm doing is sunbathing. What does it matter if I'm doing it at my house or the beach?"

She had a point and I had no answer, and she still had not opened her eyes to look at me.

"As usual, you're making something out of nothing," Eric chimed in coolly.

"Would you put some more lotion on me?" Jenna said, rolling over onto her stomach.

He knelt down and began rubbing oil on her shoulders and upper back. I wanted to knock the bottle out of his hands. Instead, I stormed off the porch, got in the car, and just started driving. It was like I was in a trance, because when I came to myself I was shocked to see that I was passing the exit for Lyndonville, Vermont, which is more than an hour from Birchfield.

It was early evening when I finally got back. I don't know where Jenna was, but Eric was sitting on the deck, clothed now, reading the paper. I told him I thought his relationship with Jenna was inappropriate, to put it mildly.

"If you're accusing me of something, I'm very hurt," he said.

All of a sudden I felt defensive, like I had done something wrong. Then it hit me. He was trying to shift the focus of the discussion from how he was with Jenna to his feelings being hurt. The bastard was trying to manipulate me.

"I'm not accusing you of anything," I shot back. "I'm telling you—as a woman and a mother. Jenna's still a child. All this attention you lavish on her is more than her years and experience can handle. She should be out with boys her own age, not doing a sex tease for her father."

"And where did you get your degree in psychology?" he responded coldly. "You talk like she's a stripper and I'm a dirty old man. Well, in case you've forgotten, she's my daughter and I'm her father and I'm also a trained psychologist. If a girl experiences her beauty with her father, her relationships with boys will be far healthier. I hate to say this, Rachel, but I think you're jealous of Jenna and jealous of my relationship with her."

There! He'd done it again! "This is not about me, Eric. It's not about my feelings for Jenna or you. Jenna's a fourteen-year-old child with breasts bigger than her brains and more hormones than common sense. You're her father, not her boyfriend. You don't have to go to bed with somebody to fuck them! Or didn't they teach you that in any of your psych courses? If I find out that you've touched her, you'll regret it for the rest of your life!"

I didn't wait to hear what, if anything, he would say back. But as I turned and walked off the porch, I thought I saw Jeremy inside

*the house moving away from the glass sliding doors. I hope he didn't
overhear us.*

I did. I'd been watching television in the family room when I
heard Mom and Dad talking loud, like they were mad at each
other. It was dark in the house and I went in the kitchen and
looked out the glass sliding doors onto the deck. I heard everything, and I understood what they were talking about because a
policeman had come to school and talked to us about what he
called "inappropriate touching" and what to do if an adult or
anybody touched us in a place they shouldn't. And I remember
when me and Mom and Dad and Jenna had watched a TV show
about a father who had abused his daughter. I heard everything
Mom and Dad said, and I got real scared. It looked like Mom and
Dad hated each other, and I wanted to say that if you guys hate
each other so much, why don't you get a divorce? But I didn't say
anything. I just went back in the family room and watched TV
and pretended like I hadn't heard anything.

I'm sorry, Mom. Maybe if I had said something, things
would be different now.

Jenna

KAREN'S HOUSE

When I woke up this morning and looked at the clock, I
freaked! It was ten-thirty! I thought I had forgotten to pull the
alarm button out last night, but then I heard music from downstairs. The Rolling Stones! Karen must be home, but at ten-thirty
in the morning?

I jumped out of bed and went to the window, and it was

snowing so hard I could hardly see the gazebo. It looked like one of those all-day snows, which meant school must have been canceled and I figured the college was closed for the day, too. I guess Karen came in and turned off my alarm so I could sleep late.

I hurried downstairs and Karen was dancing around the living room shaking her shoulders and wiggling her hips like she was auditioning to be one of Tina Turner's backup singers! And doing so in her Bill Blass silk pajamas, of course! She waved to me to join her, and we danced around the living room together until the cut—"Brown Sugar"—was over and then fell on the couch, laughing so hard we could scarcely catch our breath.

Karen likes sixties stuff as much as Dad. The Beatles are cool, but I've been trying to get her to listen to Boyz II Men and Hootie and the Blowfish. I did turn her on to Alanis Morissette, whom I've been listening to a lot since Mom died. There're days when I can hear Alanis in my head screaming, "What it all comes down to is that everything's gonna be fine fine fine." I sure hope so.

This snowstorm couldn't have come at a better time. I needed a day off on general principle, and I really needed a day off from Gregory. I was up late last night again talking to him on the phone. He'd been drinking. I can't believe his grandparents buy beer for him. His grandmother said that since he was going to drink she'd rather he stayed home and did it rather than do it at somebody else's house. I guess. I mean, that makes sense. Kind of. But I don't see why he has to drink at all. He just sits down there in his room in the basement, drinking beer, listening to Kurt Cobain, and feeling sorry for himself. His grandparents are nice, but they don't have a clue about what's going on with him. It's like they've given him a place to eat and sleep and drink, but they're too old to give him what he really needs. So guess who he's elected for that job! When I first met him, he seemed so together, and I thought we were going to help each other. That's not how it's turning out. He started hanging out with this group of kids who call themselves the Huns, and they call him Attila because of his long blond hair. I told him he was a loser if he thought the Huns were anybody to hang with. He said what did it matter what you did and who your friends were if all you were going to do was end up dead anyway? I didn't know what to say. It does matter what you do. I don't know why. It just does.

Karen made chocolate chip pancakes for breakfast, and now we're just sitting at the table. She's sipping coffee and I have a can of Coke. The snow is still coming down hard. There was at least a foot of snow on the ground already, and this new storm will probably cover the steps of the gazebo. The Weather Channel said it's going to snow until tomorrow morning. I love it when we get a snow that shuts everything down. It's incredible how something as tiny as snowflakes can bring cars, trucks, airplanes, everything to a stop! Snow is so tiny and it doesn't make a sound, and yet, we have to pay attention to it. Or maybe snowflakes do make sounds but only the trees can hear them.

I haven't gotten dressed yet. When you get dressed you feel like you have to do something, but if you keep your nightclothes on, you can't do anything except relax and take it easy. I might not get dressed ever again.

Mom would let us stay in our pajamas on snow days. She could be really silly sometimes and would dance around the house with me and Jeremy with the CD player turned up as loud as it could go, blasting a Jefferson Airplane or Grateful Dead CD. When we were tired out from that, she would play charades with us and afterward we would pop popcorn in the fireplace and she would read us a story. And then one winter snow day I stayed in my room and listened to Kurt Cobain and wondered if I would ever suffer. It sounded a lot cooler than it is.

It's nice sitting here with Karen. She lets me be. I guess Mom was like that, too, except I couldn't see it. I used to think it was really stupid the way Jeremy would sit in the kitchen with her. I used to wonder what they could be doing since they hardly ever seemed to talk. But it's like he knew something about Mom that I didn't, which is that you can't say everything with words. Maybe Mom drew and painted all the time because there weren't any words for what she wanted to say. Ever since it happened there's been so much stuff going on inside me and I don't have words for it all, but sitting here with Karen, one leg tucked under me in the chair, I feel like it's okay if I don't. At least I'm not drinking beer and listening to the depressing music of somebody who killed himself.

I look around the kitchen. It's a really nice room, kind of like our kitchen at home. Karen has a Jenn-Air stove, which is supposed to be some really big deal, and copper-bottom pots dangling from hooks on an oval, wrought-iron holder that hangs by chains from the ceiling. On the wall behind the table where we're sitting is a floor-to-ceiling case of cookbooks. You wouldn't think someone who wore Bill Blass silk pajamas would know how to boil water, but when I think about it, it makes sense. If you care about what you put on your body, you should care about what you put in it. Since I've stopped spending so much time with Gregory, I like to sit here and do my homework and watch while Karen cooks. She sharpens a knife as carefully as she puts on makeup.

Sometimes I pretend it's Mom at the stove. Other times I imagine that I'm my dad. I wonder where he sat when he lived here. And where at the table was Jenna's high chair? I wonder if Karen ever pretends that I'm her Jenna.

"Can I ask you a question?" I say, breaking the long silence.

Karen looks up. "Sure."

"It's about my dad," I feel I should add.

"That's okay."

"What was he like when you met him?"

Karen looks out the window and thinks for a moment, then shakes her head. "That was a long time ago, Jenna. Eric and I got divorced in—when was it?—nineteen-eighty-two? We met freshman year, which was—let me see—seventy-three? I'm not trying to avoid your question, but I don't remember that much."

"How could you be in love with somebody and marry them and then not remember?" I want to know.

"We remember with our emotions. The things that were important in our emotional life, that's what we remember. After we broke up, I realized that Eric's place in my feelings hadn't been as important as I'd thought. I do find myself thinking about him a lot, though, since it happened."

I take a couple of long swallows of my Coke. Mom would never have let me drink Coke for breakfast, not even on a snow day. "But I always thought you and Dad had stayed friends," I reply, putting the can on the table and turning it around and around, though I'm looking at her. "I mean, you were always at our house for holidays and birthdays and were like a second mother to me. I thought that was because you and Dad were still close and I thought it was really cool that Mom wasn't jealous."

Karen laughs. "If there was any jealousy, Eric was jealous of me and Rachel."

"Are you serious?"

Karen gets up and goes over to the counter and pours herself another cup of coffee. When she sits down again, she looks at me as if trying to decide something. "I'm not sure I want to talk about it."

"Talk about what?" I say quickly. "If there's something else awful about my family, I want to know now."

Karen reaches across the table, takes my hand, and squeezes it softly. "It's nothing like that. It's something personal. Private. And I'm not sure I'm ready to talk about it."

"Because I'm a kid?" I ask.

Karen takes a deep breath, lets it out slowly, and lets go of my hand. When she looks up at me, there are tears in her eyes. "Rachel was my best friend. We talked at least once every day, sometimes more, for fifteen years. I miss her so much. It's as if a part of me was killed and I haven't figured out yet what to do about it."

Her voice is soft, so soft I can scarcely hear her, but I do, and I am ashamed of myself. It never occurred to me that Karen might be grieving, too. "I had no idea," I admit.

"Eric asked me once if Rachel and I were lesbians."

"You're kidding! That jerk!"

"It's hard for some men to understand that women can love each other and it not be sexual. At first he thought I was trying to come between him and Rachel. In his mind, what else would we talk about except him? But Eric wasn't the center of either of our lives."

"How did you and Mom meet?"

"I met her before Eric did. When she came to the college as artist-in-residence, I interviewed her for a press release. We hit it off immediately. There was this chemistry between us, as if each of us was the sister the other had always wanted."

I shake my head and take another sip of Coke. "I don't understand. You and Mom are almost exact opposites. You're cool; she was fiery. You dress well; she cared less about clothes. I don't get it."

Karen smiles sadly. "What you saw as opposites were the very things we admired about each other. I liked her temper because there was such aliveness in it. I liked that her mind and spirit were so focused on her vision that she didn't have the time and energy to think about what to wear. And she liked having a friend who was not obsessed, who was not cursed, as she called it, to pursue a vision. I needed her because she showed me what it was to be fully alive! I am very lonely without her."

I want to tell her that she has me. Instead, I ask, "Were you jealous when Rachel and Dad started going out?"

"No. I was happy for them. Rachel wanted to know why Eric and I had divorced, of course, and I told her probably because we should never have gotten married. If my parents hadn't been killed, we probably wouldn't have. That, and if one of us had been a couple of inches shorter."

"What do you mean?"

"Neither one of us had ever been out with someone we could look in the eye. When we met freshman year, it wasn't love at first sight, but we knew we looked good together, looked like we belonged together. My concern with appearances blinded me to the fact that Eric and I had little in common. He was majoring in psych and I was an art history major, and we were great pals. But we did not share each other's passion. He would be all excited when some important psychologist would come to lecture on campus, and I didn't understand what the big deal was. And I could go to the Metropolitan Museum of Art and almost faint at the way Winslow Homer handled light in his watercolors, and Eric could've cared less. If you don't care about what makes the other feel most alive, whether you understand it or not, you shouldn't be together. But I didn't know that when I was eighteen."

"It's kind of strange that Dad married two women who were both involved in art," I comment, and finish off my Coke.

Karen nods. "I know, and I never understood what that was about. You asked me what your dad was like when I knew him. Well, the one thing that has stayed in my emotions is how he was there for me when my parents were killed. There weren't any relatives I could turn to for emotional support. Both my parents came from small families. My father had a brother but they weren't close and he didn't even come to the funeral. My mother's parents were alive but they were quite old. The only person I had was Eric, and I don't know how I would have made it through that year without him. He was my emotional anchor, very loving, very caring. He was quite remarkable for someone still in college. So when he asked me to marry him, how could I say no, given all he'd done for me? And I was lonely. There's nothing quite like the loneliness you have to live with when you don't have parents, is there?"

Tears rush to my eyes and I look down but don't say anything. I push the empty Coke can back and forth from one hand to the other until the feeling like I'm going to cry goes away. I hear the furnace click and then the little sound like a faraway wind as it begins to blow heat.

"The other thing was money," Karen continues, breaking the silence. "I inherited a lot when my parents died. Eric wanted to go to graduate school and med school and become a psychiatrist like his father. I never knew why, but Eric Senior refused to foot the bill. The money I inherited from my parents was tied up in various trusts, and I had only enough to put him through graduate school. That's why he's a psychologist and not a psychiatrist."

Karen gets up and pours her cold coffee back into the coffeemaker and lets it reheat. She's never talked to me like this, like I'm an adult. I know I'm not an adult, but kids understand a lot more than adults think. But I wonder if Karen will tell me what I really want to know.

When she comes back with her coffee, I decide to go for it. "Tell me about Jenna," I blurt out.

Karen starts, almost as if she has been bitten by something. She gives me a long stare. "How do you know about Jenna?"

"Dad told me this past summer. He said it was a secret between me and him, that Mom didn't know I was named for her."

Karen looks down as if she has found something very interesting in her coffee cup but can't figure out what it is. She turns the cup around slowly in the saucer and I feel like she's trying to decide what to say. She shakes her head slowly. "I don't know, Jenna. I don't know." She is still staring into her cup.

"You don't know what?" I ask.

"I don't know how much I should say."

"Can't you say it all?"

She looks at me. "I could, but I don't know if I should. It might be better if I waited until you're older."

I squeeze the can hard until it crumples. "There were probably lots of things Mom was going to tell me, too, when I got older."

Karen nods slowly. "You're right. You're right! There were things Rachel wanted you to know, and if something happens to me, you won't, because no one else knows them. My hesitation in telling you doesn't have anything to do with your age. I'm just afraid what I'll say will turn you against your father."

I roll my eyes. "He's doing a good job of that all by himself."

"But he's still your father. I don't want you looking back years from now and blaming me."

"That's my problem. Okay?"

"Okay."

She looks down into her coffee cup again and after a long silence, starts talking. "Jenna." She stops, then gets up and walks to the window that looks out onto the backyard and the gazebo. I wonder what she's looking at. It's snowing so hard you can't see anything except snow.

When Karen turns around there are tears in her eyes. "I sit in the gazebo sometimes and talk to her. There's a compartment in the floor of the gazebo. That's where her ashes are, in a lovely bronze Chinese urn."

"Oh, my God! Oh, my God!"

"What's wrong?" Karen wants to know.

"Oh, my God!" I repeat, feeling like an idiot because I don't know what else to say. "I'm sorry. I mean, I love that gazebo. I love to sit out there, and after Mom died, there were days when I wished it hadn't been so cold because it would've been nice to sit there. But I never knew why I liked it out there. I didn't know my sister, my half sister, was buried there."

Karen sits back down at the table. "I always thought it was odd that you liked it out there so much. I've wanted to tell you about her so many times."

"Anyway, I'm sorry but I interrupted you. You were saying—"

"She would've been nineteen this year. I still celebrate her birthday and try to imagine what she would be interested in now, what college she would be going to, and the e-mails we would send back and forth." She wipes her eyes, her head down. Without looking up, she continues. "Eric had just started working at the college when I got pregnant. Eric was ecstatic! He was so attentive to me. I had never felt so loved by him. Looking back, I realize that Eric and I were more like brother and sister. We were comfortable with each other, had fun together, but there was no passion between us. And I don't mean physically. I mean an intensity of caring about each other, the knowledge that you matter to this person more than anyone and anything on earth. I didn't feel that from Eric until I was pregnant. And it was so wonderful!

"Then the baby was born and she mattered to him and I didn't any longer. It seemed like I had only mattered because I was carrying his baby.

"Eric adored her and he'd call me from the office several times a day to ask how Jenna was doing. But he never asked how I was. I was nothing more to him than Jenna's caretaker. He didn't even see that I loved her, too. Nothing mattered except his love."

She stops, takes a deep breath, and lets it out slowly. Her head is still down and she doesn't raise it as she continues.

"It happened early spring. She was two, almost three, May eleventh. Over Eric's objections I had accepted a job in public relations at the college. I was tired of staying at home with a baby. Maybe if I had gotten some recognition for it from Eric, I wouldn't have minded as much. Maybe not at all. I loved being a mother and I also loved being out in the world. So I took the job and hired Mrs. Scarborough to take care of Jenna. Mrs. Scarborough had taken care of me when I was a baby.

"It was warm that day. Mrs. Scarborough thought Jenna was taking her nap. As it turned out, Jenna had woken up, gone down the stairs and out the front door while Mrs. Scarborough was in the kitchen chopping carrots for dinner. Eric came home to get some files he had forgotten. He was in a big hurry and sped into the driveway. It never occurred to him to look for Jenna, because she wasn't supposed to be outside. We don't know, but we think she saw his car and ran to meet him. He never saw her. He felt his car hit and roll over something. He got out and there was Jenna, dead beneath his car."

"Oh, God! Oh, my God!"

"Eric didn't tell you that part?"

I shake my head, tears in my eyes. "No. He kind of hinted that something awful had happened, but I got the feeling that it had been your fault."

"He tried to make me feel that it was. He said if I hadn't gone back to work, and hired an old woman for a nanny, it wouldn't have happened. The one thing he never said was—if he had driven slowly into the driveway like he was supposed to, it wouldn't have happened.

"That was when the marriage ended for real. Eric acted like he was the only parent who had lost a child and my grief was nothing compared to his. Grief could have brought us closer, but he wanted all the grief for himself. It was as if his world came to an end. It seemed like he was so overcome with guilt that he closed up inside and wouldn't let me or anybody get close to him.

"That's why I was so happy when he met Rachel and had a family. I thought it meant he was okay, that he'd learned to live with what had happened. But then, one Tuesday morning, he kills Rachel. I don't understand. Ever since it happened I've been trying to figure out what made him do it. I was married to the man for five years and knew him for four years before that. Would he have killed *me* if we'd stayed together? I don't think I ever really knew him. The only thing that makes sense is that something happened to him before we met. But I can't imagine what that could be."

I want to ask her to show me some pictures of Jenna, but I'm not sure I want to see them. It's weird to have a half sister who's dead. It's even weirder to think that I wouldn't be here if she had lived, because Dad and Karen might have stayed together and Dad wouldn't have married Rachel.

"Jenna?" Karen's voice breaks into my thoughts.

"Huh?"

"What was it you said Eric told you?"

"That you and he had a daughter named Jenna who died."

"And there was something else. That Rachel didn't know about Jenna?"

"No. He said Mom didn't know that I was named for her."

"I don't understand why Eric said that. Rachel knew. I know she did, because I told her. When she was carrying you, she mentioned one day that she couldn't understand why Eric was insisting on naming the baby Jenna if it was a girl. I was stunned and couldn't believe he would do that. I was pretty upset and told her. It turned out that Eric had not told her that he and I had had a child. I had never mentioned it because it's hard for me to talk about, even after all these years. But I thought Eric would have told his wife. But he hadn't."

"Holy shit!" I exclaim. "He lied to me. Why? What's up with him?" I'm so angry I want to cry as I remember that morning and my rushing to hug him and what happened.

"I don't know, Jenna. I really don't. I do know that Rachel hated the idea of you being named Jenna, and she and Eric had a huge argument about it. She wanted to name you Melissa, but when you were born, Eric told the hospital your name was Jenna and that's what was put on the birth certificate. When Rachel saw the name 'Jenna Richards' on the little name tag they put around an infant's wrist, she was hysterical and cried like I've never seen anyone cry. She felt like he had stolen you away from her."

I think I'm a little sorry I know all this now—that my dad is a liar, that he kept me and Mom from having a good relationship. But there's one more thing I have to know. I think I know the answer but I need to know for sure. "Since you and Mom were best friends, she would've told you if she was seeing somebody else, wouldn't she?"

"Yes, she would have."

"Well?"

"She was faithful to Eric from the day they met until the day she died."

My head drops and I nod glumly. "I was afraid you were going to say that. Do you have an idea why he did it?"

Karen nods. "I think so. I haven't told anyone this, so this is between us. Okay?"

I nod, wiping at my eyes.

"The day it happened, I had a meeting at nine that morning. When I came back to my office, there was a message on my voice mail from Rachel. She was very excited and said she was on her way to see Lois Finnerman, her lawyer, and had to come over to the college that afternoon and would I have time to go for a cup of coffee? I was dialing her on her cell phone when my phone rang and I was told she'd been shot. I think she was going to tell me that she was leaving Eric and taking you and Jeremy with her. I think that's why he killed her."

"Because of me?" I ask, my voice breaking.

Karen shakes her head. "No, sweetheart. It may seem like that, but that's not why."

"Then why?" I am crying now.

"I don't know, but if he had truly loved you, he could not have killed your mother. Love doesn't kill, Jenna."

I've lost it completely now, and Karen reaches across the table and grasps my hand and I let her pull me around the table and into her lap. She puts her arms around me and I cry and cry and cry. When my sobs quiet, I wipe my nose on the sleeve of my pajamas and notice that Karen is humming. I look at her but her eyes are closed and I nestle back into her arms and lay my head on her shoulder and close my eyes and I wonder if she is thinking that this could have been her Jenna. But I am her Jenna now. I'm just not that Jenna.

Jeremy

MOM'S STUDIO

I maybe should have stayed at Sara's last night. I knew it was supposed to snow today, but if I had known it was going to be this big of a storm, I would have stayed. It was snowing like crazy when I woke up, and it hasn't stopped all day. But I did bring some frozen waffles and hot dogs and cereal and milk from the house last night just in case, and it's a good thing I did. I can't open the door to get out now. Grandfather Eric called me on the cell phone to make sure I'm all right and said he'd shovel me out as soon as it stopped snowing. But I don't think that's going to be for a while.

I came home from school yesterday because I wanted to do some more work on the inventory of Mom's drawings and paintings. There're so many of them. Some are just quick sketches of different things—flowers, people sitting in DiCarlo's, trees. There're even some of the birch tree I drew! Then there're whole drawing pads filled with sketches of Jenna and me when we were little. Mom put dates on each page, and looking through them is like watching me and Jenna grow up. Other pads are filled with sketches that later became paintings. Mom was really good because she did all her sketches with pen-and-ink! I don't know how she did that.

Looking at her drawings reminds me of the Egyptian art in one of Mom's books. She said it was painted on the walls of the tombs where pharaohs were buried and was never supposed to be seen by anyone alive. Probably no one was ever supposed to see her drawing pads, either. It's like I'm an explorer who has just discovered a pharaoh's tomb!

There's one pad I don't like. It's filled with self-portraits. It seems like she did two each year, beginning with one dated right after she and Dad got married and the other on her birthday. It's a sixteen-by-twenty pad, and I put it on her easel and walk to the other end of the room. These are not sketches but complete drawings. In the sketches her line is quick, but with the drawings she worked first in pencil, very carefully, making sure each line was true, and then she used different pencils, depending on whether she wanted a dark shade or lighter one. The drawings are so lifelike. It's funny how the world is in color but an artist can draw something in pencil or pen-and-ink and make it seem more alive. That's how Mom is in her drawings of herself.

I'm jealous of Jenna because she knew Mom longer than I did. Sometimes they would talk about things that happened before I was born or before I can remember, and looking at the self-portraits Mom did before I was born or when I was little, I am sorry I never saw those faces. She looks happy and she's so beautiful. Something happened and she started to change. The line of her lip became straighter and the light in her eyes began to fade. About five years ago, her self-portraits start looking like something Picasso did. The lines are hard and there are no curves but everything is sharp angles as if she was pressing on the paper with all her strength. In one her mouth is a zipper, but in the last one, the one she did on her birthday last year, her mouth is open wide and her teeth are like a shark's and what looks like blood is coming out of her eyes.

Mom's cell phone rings.

"Hello."

"Hey, turd face."

It's Jenna! "Hi, fart breath," I answer back. I'm glad it's her but I'm a little wary. I bet she's only calling because she wants something.

"What're you doing?"

"Not much. Just watching the snow. What're you doing?"

"Not much. Watching TV, listening to CDs, talking to Karen. You know. Stuff like that."

"Yeah," I answer. I want to tell her about Mom's sketch pads, but Jenna can be friendly one day and act like she hates you the next.

"So how're you doing? It's been a long time since we talked."

That's not my fault, I want to tell her. "I'm doing okay. How're you doing?"

"I don't know. Okay, I guess."

"How's that Gregory guy?"

"He's a jerk! I don't want to talk about him."

"Well, what do you want to talk about?"

"I don't know. What do you want to talk about?"

"I don't know. You called me," I tell her.

Jenna doesn't say anything. Then I think I hear her sniffling, like she's crying. "Jen? Are you okay? What's the matter? Are you crying?"

"I miss Mom so much," she says finally, between little cries and sniffles. "Do you remember how we used to dance and play charades on snow days and keep our pj's on all day?"

"And pop popcorn in the fireplace?" I add softly.

There's another long silence, and then Jen says, "I just was wondering if you remembered."

"Yeah. I do," I answer, not wanting to cry.

"You coming for pizza Sunday?"

"Sure. I always do."

"Why don't you have Grandfather Eric bring you early, around noon or one, and we can do something?"

"Sure. If you want."

"Maybe we can build a snow-woman."

"I want to do her boobs!"

"Jeremy! You're awful!"

"And you're a fart breath."

"Turd face!"

"See ya."

"See ya."

I'm grinning as I push the End button on the cell phone and disconnect. Then I feel sad. Although I liked remembering about what snow days were like when Mom was alive, now I miss her even more. I don't know which is worse: the days I miss her a lot or the days I don't miss her at all.

I take the diary out of the bottom drawer and sit down on

the bed. I rub my hands slowly over the cover and tears come into my eyes and start trickling down my face. When they reach the corners of my mouth, I don't lick at them but let them continue to my chin, where they drop slowly onto the cover of Mom's diary.

I wish I knew what to do. There's so much to think about. Where am I going to live? Who's going to take care of me? What if Jenna and I want to do different things? And what about school? Mrs. Worthing wants me to talk to the school psychologist because I refuse to go back to my room, but I hate psychologists! Mr. Zweig is okay with me not being in my room. He meets with me a couple of times a week to go over stuff and I'm not behind in anything. But it's getting to be boring staying in the art room all the time, and I know I can't stay there with Miss Albright forever. I see everybody from my room when they come to art one afternoon each week, but I don't have much to say to them and they don't have much to say to me. Like, what would we say? But I'm going to have to go back to my room sometime.

The other thing I have to think about is Mom's paintings and drawings. What am I supposed to do with them? At first I thought it was so great that she willed them to me. But now, I wish she hadn't. I don't really know how to make an inventory. I don't know how to put on an exhibit of her paintings at some museum. I don't even know which ones are really good. But then I remember Miss Albright said Mom knew I cared about her drawings and paintings and she knew I wouldn't let anything happen to them. Mom trusted me!

SEPTEMBER 10

Eric took me to dinner last night. I can't remember the last time he took me out. We went to Nelson's, the best restaurant in town, and had Chateaubriand and an incredibly expensive bottle of red wine.

Eric was at his most charming. It was as if he knew that I'm think-ing about asking him to leave. He's very perceptive that way, which is what makes him a good therapist. It was like he was courting me again, because he had made this list of all the things he loved about me and read it to me in his most seductive voice.

If I hadn't known before that it's over, I knew last night, because I felt nothing. Just nothing. I felt like I was being manipulated. Maybe that's not fair. I don't know and I don't care. I feel dead inside to him. I just don't know if I have the courage to do anything about it.

I should have said something last night. I had been very quiet all evening. I felt sorry for him having to carry the conversation by him-self, but I had nothing to say because I didn't want to share myself with him.

We were having coffee and he asked me why I had been so silent, was everything all right? I'm such a coward. I could've said no, and maybe we could've talked about some things. But I said I was fine, that I was just absorbed in a painting I was working on, which was a lie. I haven't painted since last spring. Just sketches. Mainly I sit up there in the studio and look out the windows at the fields and won-der what happened. How did I become this unhappy woman? And why can't I do something about it?

I hate myself.

OCTOBER 25

This morning when I came back from town after my morning coffee and the paper, I went in the house. It had been so long since I'd been in the house except to cook and do laundry.

It was empty and the only sound came from the chiming clock on the mantelpiece in the family room. It was so sad remembering the first time Eric and I saw the house, with the realtor, and how excited we were the day it became ours. A home is built of the dreams you have of the kind of life you'll live inside the house. And we were so sure this house would be our home and the home to which our children would bring their children. This morning I went through each room and stood in it, remembering what was supposed to be, what is, and tried to imagine what will be.

I saved what had been our bedroom for last. I had not been in it since moving to the studio, but before I could remember if we had ever had any joy there, I noticed some letters on the nightstand.

Her name is Diane and she is a junior at the college. Eric and Diane have been seeing each other since March, and she understands that it will be a while before he "can leave Rachel because she is so psychologically unstable." Diane said that she goes to DiCarlo's some mornings and sits "where Rachel can't see me and I watch her and yes, there _is_ something disturbing about her." Diane couldn't put her finger on it, but it was obvious to her that Rachel "needs psychological counseling and it's too bad she refuses to seek it."

I wonder if Diane was one of Eric's clients, and how many other Dianes and Rachels have there been in the past fifteen years? Maybe someday I will cry, but not today. Some wounds go so deep that you don't even feel them until months, maybe years, later.

I took one of the letters, came back here to the studio, and picked up the phone. I called Lois and told her I wanted to file for divorce immediately, and we made an appointment for eleven tomorrow. Then I called President Hillman at the college, and after I told his secretary that I had evidence that someone on his staff was having a sexual relationship with a student, I got to talk to Hillman himself. I told him I had proof that Eric was sleeping with a student and I could either show it to him and the college could deal with things quietly or I could take it to the newspaper. He said he could see me at one tomorrow.

Now, all I have to do is tell Eric. I just don't know how much to tell Jen. I'm afraid I'll have to tell her everything or she'll want to go with him. Maybe talking to Karen will help. But not today. I'll call her tomorrow morning. Right now I'm too numb to talk.

SPRING

Jenna

GREGORY'S ROOM

It's a beautiful sunny day outside. The snow has almost all melted and the sunlight is changing. It's stronger than it was just a month ago, and I can't believe that I'm sitting down here listening to Greg whine.

"Life sucks, Jen. You know that? Life sucks!"

"So? What else is new?"

But I'm not sure I really believe that. I mean, it does, but it doesn't. It's like that bumper sticker says: SHIT HAPPENS. It just does and there's nothing you can do about it except wipe your butt and try to get out of the bathroom. A few months ago I would have said this to Gregory and we would have talked about it, but now what would be the point? If you don't help him feel sorry for himself, he gets pissed off and tells you that you don't understand, as if nobody has ever had the problems he does.

But if I lived in a pigsty, I'd probably think life sucked, too. I'm messy but at least my room doesn't smell! God, I don't think he's changed the sheets on that bed in a month. He got annoyed when I said I'd rather sit over here by the desk than on the bed with him. I'm afraid I'll catch a disease if I inhale too deeply. How can he make me believe he cares about me if he doesn't care about himself?

He's looking down at his hands in his lap, and I'm not prepared when he says, "My grandparents. They're going to sell the house and move to Florida."

"You're kidding!"

"I wish," he returns glumly.

"But, how could they do that?" I ask, knowing it's a stupid question but unable to stop myself from asking it.

"All the snow this winter. It was hard on them. And they've had enough."

"So what happens to you? Are you going with them?"

He shakes his head. "They're going to move into one of those retirement communities next to a golf course where they can play golf every day. No kids allowed."

"They just can't abandon you like that!" I exclaim.

He shrugs. "Sure they can. I mean, I understand. It's like they said. They raised their family and they're just too old to raise a teenager. It's not like they're kicking me out or anything. They said they'd give me some money. I have an uncle in Chicago and I can live with him. Anyway, I don't fit around here."

"That's not true," I respond, hoping I sound more convincing to him than I do to myself.

He looks up for the first time and gives me a half smile. "You don't need to lie. It's different here. You wear clothes that cost more than my dad made in a week and you don't even know it. I'm not blaming you or anything. Hey, if I had grown up here and had different parents, I'd be the same way. It's not like it's anybody's fault. That's just how it is."

Shit happens. What matters is whether you can deal with it. I am relieved that his grandparents are moving and he won't be around next year. I don't know what happened to make him change, but something did. Or maybe he didn't change that much, and it just took me a while to see that this self-pitying jerk is really who he is. At first when he'd talk about how bad he felt, I would hold him and tell him everything was going to be all right, but he'd just use that as an excuse to feel me up. He said feeling me up made him feel better. It made me feel like I was just another brand of beer. Like Alanis Morissette says: "I don't want to be a bandage if the wound is not mine," and the line I really like is "I don't want to be your food or the light from the fridge on your face at midnight."

He gets off the bed and my body stiffens as he comes toward me, but he walks by and goes to the little fridge in the corner, where he takes out a can of beer, pops it open, takes a long swig, then goes back and sits on the bed.

"Thanks for being my friend," he says. "But I guess it takes more than having dead parents for two people to be close."

"That's true," I agree. "But I'm glad you came and found me on my first day back in school. I don't know how I would've made it if you hadn't been here."

He nods. "Yeah. Me, too." He takes a sip of beer and then looks at me. His eyes are sad. "I'm sorry I've been such a jerk recently. But maybe that's the real me, you know. Maybe that's who I really am."

He's starting again. "No you aren't. Don't say that!" I feel like I'm playing a part and saying what's expected of me.

"I'm serious," he continues. "What's the point, Jen? What does it matter? I've been doing a lot of reading about suicide the past few months. Trying to understand why my dad did what he did. One book said some people kill themselves because they're angry, angry because they didn't live up to their expectations, that they're failures in their eyes or whatever. That fit my dad. He was a fuckup who said grace at every meal and went to mass every now and then. But he was still a fuckup. Sold insurance for a while, then furniture, then refrigerators, stoves, used cars, you name it, and was never good at it. My mom was a waitress. Neither one of them was going anywhere. They were just taking up space on the planet, breathing oxygen someone else could make better use of. Don't get me wrong. I loved my parents. I just was never sure if I liked them much. I would look at them and ask myself: Are these people I'd spend time with if I had a choice? And I couldn't say that they were. I hate it that I don't have a father, but when I think about *him,* there's not a lot to miss."

"I envy you," I say softly. "I didn't know there was so much to miss until after my mom was dead."

"You're lucky."

"What do you mean?"

"At least when you look back, you have things to remember. Me, I look back and all I see is my ol' man dropping me off at the soccer field, telling me he'd pick me up at four, and then driving home and doing himself in. What was he thinking when he drove me to soccer that Sunday? Was he thinking about me waiting around after the game, wondering where he was, worrying? Was he thinking about me having to bum a ride home and finding his body? What was going through that sick bastard's mind? If he wanted to kill himself, why didn't he jump in front of a bus, or stand on the train tracks, do any goddam thing rather than leave his sorry ass for me to find!"

Gregory runs a hand quickly through his hair and takes a deep swallow of beer. He's breathing hard and his eyes flit from his hands to me and back to his hands. He reminds me of a squirrel getting halfway across a street, hearing a car, and not being sure whether it wants to try to make it across or go back.

"One article I read said some people leave notes and then kill themselves in a park or someplace where a stranger will find their bodies. Some people don't leave notes and fix it so their bodies will never be found. But some don't leave notes and want to be found by someone they know. The article talked about a man who took an overdose of pills and died in bed so when his wife came home from work, she'd find him. The wife would never know why her husband did himself in and she'd probably spend the rest of her life feeling guilty, like it was her fault. The article said the husband was pissed off about something and blamed his wife, which was why she had to be the one to find his body.

"Well, that got me to thinking: What was my dad pissed off at me about? What the fuck did I do to him?"

He laughs but not like he thought of something funny. "You know why? No, I know you don't. It took me a while to figure it out. I kept trying to think of all the shit I'd done and I couldn't think of anything. I got these piercings and shit after he did himself in, so that couldn't be what pissed him off. Then it hit me. He was pissed at me because I was born. Nothing else made any sense. I don't know this for a fact, but I bet my mom got pregnant and they had to get married. I couldn't think of another reason the two of them were together. I sure as hell never felt like they loved each other. So it was my fault they ended up stuck with each other."

"That's bullshit, Gregory!"

"Then you tell me why my ol' man fixed it so I'd be the one to find his body!"

"What makes you so damned sure that's what he did? God, you're more self-centered than I am. Listen to yourself, jerk! Your dad's dead, right? Fucking dead and all you can think about is yourself!"

"What th' fuck do you know about it? You weren't there! I was!" he yells at me, his voice cracking as he fights back tears.

"Just because you were there doesn't mean you know anything!" I yell.

"Fuck you, rich bitch Jenna. Get th' fuck outta here!"

He's trying to bait me and I'm not going to let him. "No. Listen to me, Gregory." I keep my voice soft, but it is also firm. "That stuff you read about why people commit suicide? I think it's a bunch of crap."

"What th' fuck do you know, Jenna?"

"Cut it out, dammit, and listen to me, you jerk!" I shoot back, my voice rising. I wait until I'm sure he's listening. "There was this thing I saw on TV a few months back and it talked about people who are mentally ill, and it said that mental illness is kind of like cancer or something like that except it's happening in your mind and you might not be responsible for what you do. I think your dad had an illness in his head. I don't think he thought about who would find his body or anything like that. I think he was hurting so bad in his head that all he was trying to do was make the hurting go away. I don't think what your dad did had anything to do with you." I'm not sure about my dad, but I don't say anything about that.

Gregory is staring at his hands, and I think I see a tear drop from the end of his nose and into his lap. "I know it's hard," I continue, my voice almost a whisper, "but maybe, maybe you'll feel sorry for your dad one of these days."

"Do you feel sorry for yours?" he asks. His voice is soft now, too, and he looks up at me and I see the tears glistening on his face.

"No," I whisper. "I used to think I did. At the beginning. But I was just trying to cover up how angry I was at him. But when I used to go see him, it was like visiting somebody I didn't know. He looked like my dad, but that was all. I think when he shot Mom that he killed himself, too."

"I know what you mean, except I feel like I'm hanging on the rope with my dad." He turns up the beer can, drains it, and throws the empty can in the direction of the wastebasket, which is almost overflowing with empty cans. He misses and the can falls onto a pile of dirty clothes. He gets another beer from the fridge, walking by without looking at me, and returns to the bed.

"Maybe you're right, Jen. Maybe he wasn't well in the head

and didn't think about that I would be the one to find the body. But that still doesn't change one thing."

"What's that?"

"The thing that made me stop giving a damn about anything but getting drunk. There was this other article I read that said that the children of people who commit suicide are in danger of killing themselves when they reach the age of the parent who committed suicide. Something about they'll feel guilty if they live longer than the parent who died. So if I'm going to kill myself when I get to be forty-one, then what's the point? I might as well drink and screw around until my time is up."

"That is just about the stupidest thing I've ever heard!" I explode in disgust.

"Just because something's stupid doesn't mean it's not true."

"And that's the second stupidest thing I've ever heard."

"Well, if I have said the two most stupid things you've ever heard, that must mean that I'm the stupidest person you've ever met."

"Gregory, stop it! Just stop it! What's with all the self-pity crap?"

"If I don't feel sorry for myself, who will? Listen, Jen. Your mother left you a pile of money and a house. Karen took you in without blinking an eye. My father didn't leave me enough to buy a stamp, and my mother didn't leave me enough spit to lick the stamp if my father had left one, and I don't have any friends of the family living in big houses lined up at the sign that says 'Gregory Needs a Home.'"

His voice is quiet but he is looking straight at me and his eyes are hard and cold. For the first time I see that he hates me. "I've got to go study for the algebra midterm," I say, getting up and putting on my coat.

"Jen? Stop. I'm sorry," he apologizes, his eyes softening. "You're right. I do get caught up in feeling sorry for myself. I apologize for what I said about you having it made. That wasn't right."

"That's okay," I say, standing in the doorway. "But I do have to study for that midterm. Talk to you." I hate to leave him here by himself, but all I know is that I've got to get out of here before he drags me down some more. I hurry up the stairs and into the kitchen and ask his grandfather for a ride.

Jeremy

MOM'S STUDIO

I've just about finished the inventory of Mom's paintings. I stopped for a while because it was too hard. But I figured out I was having a hard time because I thought I had to get it done all at once. But I don't. I just have to do one at a time.

Mom hadn't named a lot of them, so that was the hardest part. She said it was easier for her to paint them than name them. When she did name them, she used simple ones, like *Morning on the Town Common.* So that's what I did for the ones I had to put names to.

I've learned so much about art from doing this. I thought I was good because I can draw faces and almost anything I see, but Mom and Miss Albright draw in a way that it makes you wonder who the people are and what they're thinking. And even when there're no people in their drawings and paintings, you feel something when you look at them. I don't know how to do that. Mom has pads filled with sketches of people drinking coffee and reading the paper, walking across the town common, sitting on the grass or on benches.

I see how she took different sketches and put them together in a painting. I love the way she worked with the light—the direction the light was coming from, and if it was a pale morning light or bright afternoon or deep evening. I spend a lot more time now watching how the light changes and how it's different shining on the few remaining patches of snow or if it's on the bare ground next to the snow. What I haven't figured out is how to draw and paint so someone else will see it and know if it was morning, afternoon, or evening.

I hear a knock at the door. Who could that be? Grandfather Eric left early this morning. I go down the stairs.

"Jeremy!" a voice calls through the door.

"Jenna?"

"Open the door, fart face!"

I am grinning as I unlock the door and open it. "Hi, turd breath!"

She is grinning, too, as she comes in. "What're you doing?"

"Nothing," I say, closing the door behind her. "What're you doing here?"

"Oh, I was at the 'Gregory guy's' house and I was going to go home but then I thought you might be around and told his grandfather to drop me off here. There's no law that says we can only see each other on Sundays, is there?"

I smile. "Nope, and Saturday's close to Sunday, anyway."

"That's what I thought."

Jenna is standing in the middle of the room looking around as if she's never been here. Her face is sad, and I think she's been crying. She flops down on the couch and I go sit at the other end.

"God, this is strange," she says, frowning. "This is the first time I've been over here since the day after it happened, the day I picked up my clothes. And I can't remember the last time I was in the studio. You hungry?"

I shrug. "Sure. I had some cereal when I got up, but that's been about it."

"Is Grandfather Eric in the house?"

"Naw. He left early this morning to go see Dad's lawyer. I'll be glad when the trial starts."

"Me, too. June. Two more months."

"What if he gets off? Like O. J. Simpson did!"

Jenna shakes her head. "This is different. Nobody saw O. J. Simpson do it. Dad did it in broad daylight in the center of town."

"I forgot about that."

"Well, I'm starving! Let's go get something to eat."

I lock the door behind me, feeling how nice it is to be able to walk the short distance from the studio to the house without putting my jacket and hat and mittens on.

"Why did you lock the door?" Jenna asks, frowning.

"I don't want anyone going in there and messing with Mom's things." And her diary, I add silently to myself. I expect Jenna to say something sarcastic, but she doesn't.

We find some frozen dinners in the fridge and put them in the microwave.

"You want a Coke?" Jen asks.

"Sure."

"I don't see how you can stay here," Jenna says once the food is ready and we're sitting at the table.

"What do you mean?"

"It's so creepy. I still expect Mom or Dad to walk in any minute."

"Yeah, I know. But I kind of like it."

"You do?"

"Kind of. I mean, it's hard sometimes. I think I see Mom standing at the stove making soup and then realize that I only imagined it."

"She made the best soups of anybody in the world! You remember the one she used to make with cheddar cheese and beer?"

138

"Oh, wow! I'd forgotten about that! It was awesome!" I exclaim.

"She put it in the big blue soup tureen—"

"And she'd bake some French bread—"

"That was the best!"

We are quiet for a minute. "Sometimes it hurts to remember," I say, breaking the silence. "But other times it helps."

"It's probably easier for you. You were close to Mom. You were her favorite and I was Dad's."

"I guess," I say quietly. But after reading Mom's diary, I'm not sure.

We talk about school stuff until we're done eating, and clean up.

"What do you want to do?" I ask.

"I don't know. What do you want to do?"

"What we're doing is okay with me."

"Just hanging out?"

"Yeah. Just hanging out."

"Then let's go back to the studio. You're used to being in the house but I'm not and it's kind of creepy being in here. And I don't want to be here when Grandfather Eric shows up."

"What's up?" I ask her, as we go out the back door. "I thought the two of you were, well, you know." I don't want to say that I thought the two of them were lovey-dovey because they were on Dad's side.

Jenna doesn't say anything until we're back in the studio, door locked, and we're stretched out at opposite ends of the couch.

"Has Dad's lawyer talked to you?" she asks.

"Yeah. He wanted me to testify at Dad's trial that Mom used to fight with him."

"What did you say?"

"Nothing. I told him I didn't remember. And, anyway, Mom never fought Dad. She slapped him that one time and that was all."

"So are you going to testify?"

I wonder if this is why she's here. I should've known. The lawyer and Grandfather Eric told her to come talk to me and convince me to testify. "No." I want to ask her if she's testifying, as if I don't already know, but I don't want to hear her say it.

"Dad said that if we both testified he might get a lighter sentence. He said the jury would believe it if his children said that Mom hit him and fought with him a lot."

"But that's not how it was!" I protest.

"Dad said it was important for the jury to hear how Mom fought with me all the time."

"You fought with her a lot more than she did with you!" I am starting to get upset.

"I know," Jen says quietly. "I know. It was always stupid stuff, too. She'd say something, and I'd pick up on her tone of voice and think she was criticizing me when she was really trying to help me, or she'd say something and I would sigh or roll my eyes and she'd think I was criticizing her and next thing I knew we'd be yelling at each other. God, I hated it! I hated it so much! But I couldn't help it."

"I think you and Mom were a lot alike."

"You do?" she says, looking at me, her eyes getting big.

"Maybe that's why you argued so much. You *think* you're like Dad, but that's not true. I think I'm more like Dad, unfortunately."

"What do you mean?"

"Well, you and Mom always said what you felt. But me and Dad, we think a lot. We don't say anything until we've thought about it."

"Oh, wow! You are so right! I never thought of that, but you are so right!"

"Sometimes I wished Mom would have yelled at me like she did you."

"Are you serious? God, and I wished I could've hung around with Mom the way you did."

"I guess I hung out with her so much because I wanted to be close to her and didn't know how. All we talked about mostly was art. I think I started drawing because that seemed to be what mattered the most to her. But it seemed like everything you did mattered to her—what you wore, how you fixed your hair, where you went. Mom noticed you. She only noticed me when I was drawing."

Jenna is looking at me like she can't believe I just said all that. I can't either, since I didn't know I knew that until it came out. But I've been thinking about it a lot since reading Mom's diary. I kept hoping that my name would be in there, that Mom would write something nice about me. But except for the day when she moved out of the house, she hardly mentioned my name. But Jenna! She worried about Jenna.

"But Mom left all her drawings and paintings *and* the studio to you."

"Her art. I know."

"But her art was also her. She left you the most important part of herself."

I hadn't thought of it that way. "I guess she loved both of us, but in different ways."

Jenna nods. "Yeah. That's it. Isn't it funny how I wanted her to love me the way she did you and you wanted her to love you the way she did me?"

Our legs are touching and it feels real nice to be lying here with her like this, and I am afraid that if I ask, the feeling will go away. But I can't enjoy the feeling if I don't know.

"Are you going to testify at Dad's trial?" I ask, my voice shaking a little.

"No."

"You aren't?" I'm almost shouting.

"I aren't," she says, smiling. "Fooled you, huh?"

"Uh-huh. You really aren't going to testify? For real?"

"For real. I stopped going to see Dad because that's all he wanted to talk about. Grandfather Eric and the lawyer were calling me at Karen's all the time, and she had to tell them to stop or she was going to tell the newspaper they were harassing me."

"How's—how's Dad?"

"Last time I saw him, which was back in February, he was in pretty bad shape. He'd lost a lot of weight and was real depressed."

"Did he say why he did it?"

"No."

"Why aren't you going to testify? I thought you were on his side."

She shrugs. "God, I don't know what I was. I was so confused. I didn't know what to believe until Karen told me that Mom wasn't doing anything with another man. That and something else I don't want to talk about. That's when I knew for sure that Dad was lying. You can say, 'I told you so,' if you want."

I shake my head. "No. That's all right." I don't want to make Jen feel bad. I'm just glad she's here.

"So what's going to happen to us?" she asks, breaking the silence. "The trial is the first of June and then a couple of weeks later, school's out. What then? You probably want to go live in San Francisco with Gran and Grampy."

"Maybe," I say, "but I don't know. I think about it a lot. Part of me wants to go there and part of me doesn't."

"If that's what you really want to do, that would be okay with me. Gran and I would yell at each other a lot, but she would also buy me whatever I wanted. But you know what scares me?"

"What?"

"What if something happens to them? They're both in their sixties. What if one or both of them died? Or maybe they'll decide they want to go live in Florida next to a golf course. Then where would we be?"

"But why would they want to go live in Florida?"

"I don't know. Because they're old."

"I don't know what to do. Once the trial is over, Grandfather Eric'll probably go back to Pennsylvania. Then I won't be able to stay here anymore."

"You can come stay at Karen's."

"I know, but what about the house and the studio and Mom's paintings? I can't just leave them here."

"We're too young to have to think about crap like this!" Jen explodes. "I hate his guts! I really hate his fucking guts!"

Jenna bursts into tears, and quickly I move to the other end of the couch and put my arms around her. Her head burrows into my shoulder and I can feel snot getting on my sweater but I don't care.

Jenna

School

THE CAFETERIA

"... such a creep. *And the harder he tries not to be, the more of one he is...*"

Gregory hasn't been to school since I saw him last weekend. I call his house every day, but his grandfather says they haven't seen him and I can tell that he isn't heartbroken.

"... *was dying, just dying to go see No Doubt when they were in Boston. You'd think my mom would've understood, with her always telling me how she was at Woodstock and had Jimi Hendrix, whoever he is, autograph her tits, but nooooo! She had to spend the whole weekend writing briefs for some case so she can become partner at her law firm...*"

It's kind of like Gregory died, because I know he's not here but I look for him every time I come in the cafeteria. I go by his locker a couple of times a day when I know he's supposed to be there. I miss him. Well, maybe not him, but somebody who knows what it's like. Somebody besides Jeremy. I sit here at a table with Liz and Janie and Gwen, who I've known since elementary school. We used to talk about everything, and now, they don't know what to say to me and I don't know what to say to them. We try to act like nothing has changed, but we all know it has. I'm just not interested in the things they are, and I can't stand sitting here nibbling at my salad and listening to them bitch about their parents. But this is what I used to sound like. Now I want to say to them, "You *have* parents and so what if they're clueless? Big deal. At least they're there! Can't you look at me and understand that much?"

"... *hypocrites! They want to ground me for a week just because they found a roach in the pocket of my jeans. They wanted to know where I got it from and who taught me how to do it. They are so ridiculous. I finally looked at my dad and said, 'I got it from the stash you keep hidden in the back of your closet.' He almost shit a brick. It's okay for him and Mom to light up, but they now have the nerve to tell me I can't? Bullshit!*"

This morning while I was waiting for my bagel to toast, I was leafing through Karen's *Paris Vogue,* which came yesterday, and there was a photo in an ad of a girl in a bridal gown, and I started daydreaming about when I get married and Mom helping me get dressed the morning of the wedding and Dad walking me down the aisle, and suddenly it was like somebody kicked me in the stomach and slapped my face at the same time. I didn't know just how much a part my parents were of every daydream I've ever had about my life—going to college, getting married, having children, probably getting divorced, getting a job, and getting married again.

I start daydreaming about the eighth-grade dance, and I see Mom and Dad telling me how pretty I look. It's like from now on every happy event of my life is going to be sad, too. I know how Gregory feels, because sometimes I feel like why should I bother to go on? Larry Sullivan asked me to go to the eighth-grade dance with him, and I didn't even have to think about it. I just said no. Karen tried to get me to change my mind, but I didn't. Maybe I will regret not going, like she said, but that'll be easier to deal with than going to the dance and pretending to be feeling stuff that I'm not feeling and not being able to let out my real feelings.

I don't realize that I'm standing up with my tray in my hand until I hear Liz say in that fake voice of concern she seems to have invented just for me, "What's up, Jenna? Where're you going?"

I have no idea. I just need to get away from here. "Uh, nothing," I mumble. "Just thought of something I have to do."

Liz gives me a look that's supposed to make me feel like she understands. She doesn't, but I can't get angry at her. I wouldn't know how to deal with me, either. I used to be Miss Bad-Ass-Foul-Mouth and now I hardly say a word to anybody and get straight As in all my classes.

After putting my tray away, I wander out of the cafeteria. I'm passing the auditorium on my way to the library when I notice a plaque on the wall next to the main doors. I go over and look at it.

IN MEMORY OF THE GRADUATES
OF MARTIN LUTHER KING JR. MIDDLE SCHOOL
WHO GAVE THEIR LIVES IN THE VIETNAM WAR:

WILLIAM ALBERT LEWIS JR.
ROGER THOMAS SIMMONS
ELIJAH WILLIAMS III

Has this been here all the while and I never saw it until today? Or did I see it and it didn't mean anything to me? I can't believe I've been walking past this for almost two years and never paid any attention to it.

I wonder who they were. It's weird to think that they walked up and down these same halls and who knows? I might've sat in the same seat as one of them did in English or Algebra, or the cafeteria. They were kids just like us. And now they're dead.

But in a way they aren't. I'm standing here thinking about them, wondering who they were and what was it like for them when they were my age. Maybe as long as somebody can read your name somewhere and wonder about you, then you can't be dead. Not all the way dead.

Like the AIDS Quilt I saw on TV. It was amazing! It wasn't just the names of people who'd died of AIDS, but those who sewed the squares put things on them to give you a feeling about the person. I remember one had a guitar and musical notes on it to let you know that he had liked music, and another one had orchids on it and I guess that man liked orchids or maybe even raised them.

It was sad thinking about those people not being around any- more to make music for somebody to listen to and grow orchids for somebody else to smell. But looking at the squares, I could imagine the music that man would've made and imagine the or- chids the other man would've raised, which meant they weren't all the way dead.

It would be so cool if there was something like the AIDS Quilt for everybody whose mom or dad died while they were children. It could have our names and the name of the parent who'd died on it. For Mom's square, I'd put a soup bowl and a ladle. But what would be even better than a quilt would be if we could all meet someplace that was really beautiful, like Golden Gate Park in San Francisco, and we could tell each other stories about our parents and just be with each other and not have to pretend to care about stuff we didn't care about anymore and then maybe we wouldn't be lonely because we'd know other kids like us and we could call and talk to each other when we needed somebody to understand what it was like to do stuff without your mom or dad there to tell you how proud they were of you! But we could send each other e-mails and talk about how happy and how sad we were at the prom or whatever.

That's it! That's it! I'm a fucking genius!! There *is* a place where something like that can happen. What if I started a web site where kids could put up pictures of the parent who died and write things about them? It would be like this incredible quilt, except you wouldn't have to make a trip someplace to see it. No matter where you were, it would be there. Maybe kids from places like Kosovo and Northern Ireland who've had parents killed in wars would write stuff, and it wouldn't matter if you couldn't read the language they were writing in because you'd know, you'd just know, what they were saying.

I can't believe I got such a great idea! I don't know anything about computers but Jeremy does, and that little girl whose house he stays at all the time—Sara—her dad owns a computer store! I bet he could help!

Jeremy

SARA'S HOUSE

Dad's trial starts next Monday. For the past couple of weeks I've been living at Sara's. Grandfather Eric is letting Dad's lawyer stay at the house. It wasn't only going in the house to get something to eat and seeing Dad's lawyer sitting around the kitchen, smoking and with papers spread all over the table. One day I came home after school and as I started up the driveway, a man took my picture and then started asking me how I felt about my dad and was I going to the trial?

I ran inside the studio and called Bob. He had given me his phone number at work and said I could call anytime I wanted to. I was crying and he left his store and came and got me. That was when he said I could stay here as long as I wanted.

I like it here. Elaine reminds me of Mom a little, because she bakes bread and makes thick soups sometimes. Bob is nothing like Dad, though. He has a black beard and is always smiling. I want to ask him why he's so happy. Maybe that's just how he is. Some people are born happy and some people aren't. Jen was born happy. I'm not sure about me yet.

It's kind of strange but nice to be sitting here at the dinner table—me, Sara, Bob, Elaine, and Jenna. This is the first time Jen's been here. If anybody looked in through the window over the sink, they would think we were a family. Jen wanted to come over to ask Bob to help her with her idea for a web page for kids whose parents have died. I told her she couldn't curse around Sara and she said okay.

I wasn't sure how Sara would feel about Jen coming for dinner, but she seems pretty happy, like she now has a big "sister" to go with her big "brother," me. Jenna and Bob have been talking and even though both his parents are still alive, he seems as excited about the web site as Jenna. They go into the family room, where there's a computer, leaving me, Sara, and Elaine sitting at the table.

"Do you miss your mother?" Sara asks.

"Sara! You aren't supposed to ask Jeremy that. Remember?" Then she turns to me. "I'm sorry. I know that you told her your mother had died, but ever since you started coming here last fall she wanted to know what happened. She was very concerned because she said you seemed very sad and that was why she went up to you in Miss Albright's room that day. So we thought it best to tell her what happened. But she promised not to bring it up to you."

"It's okay," I respond. I look at Sara. "Yes. I miss my mother."

"My mom will be your mother. Won't you, Mom?"

Elaine blushes. She doesn't know what to say. Neither do I. Our eyes meet and then we both look away.

"Think about it, Mom. Okay?" Sara says, breaking the awkward silence. "Would you like my mom to be your mom?" Sara asks me.

I want to say yes, but what if I do and Elaine doesn't want to? But before I know it, my mouth says, "That would be great."

Sara's face breaks into a big grin. "What do you say, Mom?"

Elaine smiles. "Your father and I will have to talk about it."

"But I heard you talking about it one day and Dad said—"

"Sara! That's enough. Why don't you two go find something to do while I clean up."

"I can help," I offer.

"Go. I'll be fine."

I can't believe it! Maybe Bob and Elaine want to adopt me. But I don't know if they can. I mean, what do you have to do to adopt somebody? It's probably real hard, and what about Grampy and Gran? They will probably say Jen and I have to come live with them. Sometimes I feel like a homeless person. I have places where I can go and sleep, but that's not the same as a home. A home is a place where you're always wanted.

Sara and I go into the family room.

"Jeremy! Bob is showing me how to create a web page!"

Sometimes Jenna makes me angry! She hasn't been here an hour and already she's calling people by their first names and hogging the computer.

"What do you think, Jeremy?" Bob turns and asks me, nodding at the computer screen.

At the top of the screen are the words *The Haven*. Underneath in smaller letters it says, "A place for children whose parents have died."

"So? Say something," Jenna prods me.

"I'm thinking," I answer slowly, trying to stay mad at her but getting interested in what she and Bob are doing.

"So what're you thinking, Jeremy?" Bob wants to know.

"About what it looks like. What if the words *The Haven* were curved, like in a semicircle?"

"An arc!" Bob responds, excited. He does a couple of quick clicks on the computer mouse and, like magic, the two words are now in a semicircle. "Like that?"

"Yeah! And then, maybe a design or a picture and then, below that you could put 'A place for children whose parents have died.'"

"What do you think should go in the middle?"

"Maybe some flowers," Jen offers. "Wait a minute! Jeremy! You remember a couple of summers ago when we went to California and Mom took us somewhere. It was north of San Francisco, I think."

"Oh yeah! I remember that!"

"Do you remember seeing fields of purple wildflowers?"

I nod, excited now, too. "They looked so pretty in the green grass."

Bob clicks on the mouse some more and begins showing us nature photographs.

"Like that!" Jen exclaims, pointing to a photograph that is almost exactly like what we saw.

"That's it!" I agree. The flowers are the same ones as on the cover of Mom's diary.

A few more clicks and the photograph is on the web site. Bob moves the other words beneath the picture.

"That's awesome!" Jen exclaims, looking at me. "Great idea! It looks so peaceful and inviting now."

"What next?" Bob wants to know.

Jen shakes her head. "I don't know. I've been going back and forth in my head about this and had almost decided it was too crazy an idea, but seeing it on the screen, I'm so excited I can't think straight."

"That's fine. I'll save it and the next time you and Jeremy want to work on it, just let me know. It'll be here."

"Thank you so much!" Jen says. "So, so much!"

She gets up from the chair where she's been sitting next to Bob.

"I'll take you home whenever you're ready," he offers.

"Thanks. I need to talk to my brother for a minute and then I'll be ready to go."

"Take your time."

Jen and I go into the living room and sit on the couch.

"Thanks, Jeremy. You really have a good eye for stuff like this."

I shrug. "I guess."

"Will you help me put it together?"

"If you want me to."

"I want you to."

I smile. "Then, sure."

We're quiet for a minute. I think I know what she wants to talk about. I want to, too.

"Are you going to the trial?" she asks.

I nod. I have to. I want to tell her why, but I can't. "Are you going?"

She nods. "Part of me wishes it was all over with. I mean, I keep thinking, what if the jury says he's not guilty and he gets out of jail? Would that mean we'd have to go back and live with him?"

"No way!" I exclaim. "No way! How could a jury say he didn't do it when everybody knows he did? That doesn't make sense!"

"I know. But I guess it could happen. Anyway, Karen said the prosecutor wants to meet with you and me."

"Why does he—"

"She."

"Why does she want to meet with us?"

"Just to let us know what's going to happen. She said the trial shouldn't take more than a day or two since there's no question that Dad did it. The only thing that needs to be decided is if he was crazy when he did it."

"He wasn't. I know he wasn't."

"How can you be so sure?"

"I just am."

"You're probably right. Anyway, the prosecutor is coming over to Karen's Friday after Grampy and Gran get into town. Okay?"

"Sure."

Jen gets up. "It's really nice here. Elaine and Bob are nice, too. You're lucky and I'm kind of jealous."

"What do you mean?"

"Living with Karen is cool, but it's like we're roommates. You're lucky."

Bob asks if I want to ride with them. I shake my head.

"See ya," Jen says, and she wouldn't say it in front of Bob and Sara, but I can hear her add "fart face."

"See ya," I reply, and silently add "turd breath."

We smile at each other as she goes out the door.

Jenna

Friday we met with Gloria Miller, the prosecutor. She said she would have police cars bring us to court today, and they would take us in through a back entrance so we wouldn't have to talk to any reporters. When she said it I thought it was a stupid idea. So what if there were a few reporters around?

I couldn't believe it when we drove up this morning. There were tons of TV cameras set up out front, and I thought I recognized Audrey Perkins from Channel 6! She was interviewing Grandfather Eric and Aaron Mitchell, Dad's lawyer. While I wouldn't have minded seeing myself on TV tonight, I'm glad we didn't have to walk by all those reporters and cameras.

The courtroom is smaller than the ones on television. The judge's bench is to the left of where we're sitting. The place where the jury sits is to our right and directly across from the judge. There are two tables. Dad and Aaron Mitchell sit at the one closest to the judge. Gloria sits at the one directly in front of us. There're only about four rows on each side of the courtroom for spectators and most of those are filled with reporters. However, nobody else sits in the first row with me, Jeremy, Karen, Grampy, and Gran. On the other side of the aisle, behind the table where Dad is, Grandfather Eric sits by himself. I feel kind of sorry for him but not sorry enough to go sit with him.

Jeremy looks serious. He's staring straight ahead and clutching the backpack Mom made for him on his lap as if there's gold or diamonds inside. I asked him why he brought it but all he said was "Because." Sometimes he acts real smart and sometimes he acts like he's totally dumb.

When Dad was brought in by two guards, Jeremy gasped. Dad looks even thinner than the last time I saw him, this past winter, and he looks old. There's gray in his hair and his face is tight, like there's a string inside and somebody is pulling it. He didn't look at us. I feel kind of weird that he didn't, but then I think I would've felt weird if he had.

The jury is coming in, and I look at them and try to tell what they might be thinking and what they will decide about Dad. There're eight women and four men, and there's one big fat man whose hair is parted in the middle who looks like he would find his own mother guilty of something.

Things are moving along pretty fast. Gloria and Dad's lawyer start by telling the jury what each is going to prove. Gloria says the evidence will show that Dad was fighting with Mom in front of Sutter's, took out a gun, and shot her in the face twice. Why he did it didn't matter. "Nobody deserves to be shot in cold blood in the middle of the street at ten o'clock in the morning."

Aaron Mitchell is tall and blond and has a deep voice. He looks like a TV anchorman, and I bet if anybody can get Dad off, he can. He says the reasons *do* matter, that Dad was a battered husband who had been abused by Mom for years and had been pushed to a point where he snapped. All the while he's talking, though, Jeremy is muttering under his breath, "Liar. Liar. House on fire. Liar." He'd better keep quiet. Gloria told us that Judge Livingstone doesn't like talking in her courtroom.

After Dad's lawyer finishes, the first witness is called. It's somebody who testifies about talking with Mom in Sutter's that morning and seeing her walk out of the store. The next person says he was coming down the street toward Sutter's and saw Dad talking to Mom, saw him pull at her arm like there was something she had that he wanted, and then pull out a gun and shoot her in the face two times. Then, the man said, Dad reached down, and it looked like he took something out of Mom's bag or maybe one of her pockets, and ran away.

Gloria turns to Dad's lawyer and says, "Your witness."

Aaron Mitchell says, "No questions."

After that, the policeman who was the first to find Mom testifies about what he saw. When he starts describing the bullet holes and what they looked like, both Jeremy and I cover our ears. Gloria shows the jury some photographs of Mom lying on the sidewalk, and Jeremy and I put our heads down. We aren't close enough to see anything, but that doesn't matter.

Aaron Mitchell doesn't have anything to ask him, either.

Then another policeman talks about going to the house and finding Dad sitting on the front porch with a gun in his hand, saying he had shot his wife and was going to kill himself.

Next comes someone who says Dad's gun was the one that killed Mom. Somebody else testifies that he gave Dad some kind of test that showed he had fired a gun recently.

Then Reverend Edwards talks about what a good person Mom was, and after her, an art critic from New York talks about what an important artist she was. After he finishes, Gloria says, "The prosecution rests, your honor."

Judge Livingstone is young looking. She says that because the defense had no questions for any of the state's witnesses, that things are moving quickly and she wants to know if the defense is ready to put on its case. Aaron Mitchell says he only has three witnesses.

The first two are psychiatrists who talk about something called battered husband syndrome. It doesn't make sense to me. It's not like Mom was beating him up like some men do women. But both psychiatrists say Dad was afraid of Mom, afraid she was going to leave him for somebody else. Sure, Mom yelled a lot, but that was just her. She could yell one minute and be fine a couple of minutes later. That was one good thing about Mom. When she was angry, she let you know it and then it was over with.

Dad has just been sworn in and is sitting in the witness chair. He still doesn't look at us, but turns partway toward the jury and he's smiling just a little bit. It's like he's trying to charm the jury. He crosses his legs and from looking at him you'd never know he'd shot somebody. He doesn't look like a murderer. God, I bet he's going to talk his way out of this.

"Dr. Richards, would you begin by telling us something of your background?" his lawyer asks.

"Certainly. I have a bachelor's degree in psychology and a Ph.D. from Columbia. I have published widely in a number of psychology journals and given papers at conventions."

"Where were you employed?"

"I was chief psychologist at Birchfield College for almost twenty years. And I also have—had—a small private practice."

"And clients came to see you from places other than just Birchfield?"

"Yes. I had clients who came from Montreal and several over the years who would fly up once a week from New York to see me."

"When did you meet Rachel Pierce?"

"Rachel and I met in nineteen-eighty. She was artist-in-residence that year, and we met at the opening of an exhibition of her work. We seemed to like each other and I invited her out for a drink, as I recall, and things developed from there."

"And how soon after that did you marry?"

"Two years later."

"Why the long wait?"

"Well, I had observed signs of what seemed to be psychological instability in her."

"Such as?"

"Her moods. One minute she could be very angry and the next she would be like nothing had happened. Quite frankly, her temper frightened me. She could fly into rages that were terrifying. After we had children, she would go into these tirades against our daughter, and poor Jenna would come to me, crying."

"That's a fucking lie!" I whisper to Jeremy.

"Objection!" Gloria shouts, jumping to her feet.

"Sustained," the judge says.

"What just happened?" Jeremy wants to know.

"I'm not sure. I think the judge said Dad couldn't talk about me. Especially since that never happened."

"Then tell the judge," Jeremy says. "Tell her."

"You can't do that in a trial, Jeremy. Shh. I want to hear what Dad's lawyer is saying."

"Did your wife seek psychological or psychiatric help?"

"I begged her to, but she couldn't see that she had a problem."

"And yet, you married her?"

Dad looks at the jury and smiles. "I loved her. And I thought that over time I would be able to help her. I also thought that having children would work a change on her over time."

"Did anything change?"

"Unfortunately, no. It was as if she now had another target for her unbelievable rages."

"And who was that?"

"Our daughter. I became fearful for our daughter's emotional health and developed a very close relationship with her to protect her from Rachel."

Dad is looking just at his lawyer as he says this. I think he's afraid to look at me and say that.

"You have a son?"

"Yes. I was afraid for him also, because he was so close to his mother. The two were inseparable. I didn't think it was a healthy relationship, but I did not intervene for fear that he would turn against me."

"Did you have other fears?"

"Well, yes. It is difficult to say this and I was ashamed for even thinking it then, but I wondered if she might be abusing him sexually."

"No way!" Jeremy says under his breath.

"Your honor!" Gloria screams, jumping to her feet. "This is outrageous!"

"Your honor," Aaron Mitchell says calmly, "the witness is not asserting that his wife was abusing their son. He is testifying to his fear. His statement goes to his state of mind."

"I'll allow it," the judge says.

"Your honor," Gloria begins in a pleading voice.

"Sit down, counselor."

This is bullshit! I can't believe the judge is going to let him get away with saying stuff like that. He's lying, and Jeremy and I are the only ones who know it. But we can't say anything or the judge will throw us out. I've never seen Jeremy so upset. He's mumbling to himself and clenching his fists. I grab his hands and squeeze them tightly to try and calm him down.

"What led you to think your wife might be abusing your son?" Dad's lawyer continues.

"This past summer she moved out of the house and into her studio, a barn we had converted into a wonderful space in which she could paint. She moved her things out there and announced she was going to be living there from now on. And, to my consternation, Jeremy, our son, began sleeping out there also. I seldom saw either of them anymore, except at dinnertime."

"What happened that morning last October?"

"The children had left for school. I was sitting in the kitchen going over some case files of students I would be seeing that day when Rachel walked in. I was surprised. Rachel has always been a late sleeper and so for her to be up and about at eight o'clock in the morning was unusual. She said that we needed to talk. Then she proceeded to tell me that she wanted me out of the house by five o'clock that evening, that she was filing for a divorce. When I asked her why, she said that she had fallen in love with someone else. I wanted to know who. She wouldn't tell me, but finally she admitted that it was another woman."

I gasp aloud and just as I do, Jeremy pulls his hands out of mine and leaps to his feet and starts shouting, "That's a lie! That's a lie!"

"Order! Order in the court!" the judge shouts, banging her gavel.

"I can prove it. He's lying! He's lying! I have proof! He's lying!" Jeremy shouts at the top of his voice, tears pouring down his face but staring straight at Dad. Frantically he reaches inside his backpack and pulls out a book with flowers on it, flowers like the ones on the web page.

"I have proof!" he says again, and holds up the book.

"What is that, young man?" the judge wants to know.

"My mom's diary. It proves that he's lying!"

Dad's lawyer jumps up and starts shouting, "Objection! Objection!" and Gloria is on her feet shouting something, which I can't hear because everybody in the courtroom is talking. Dad's mouth is hanging open and he's staring at Jeremy like he wants to kill him. I can't see Jeremy's face, but I think he's staring back at Dad in the same way. Grampy has put his hand on Jeremy's shoulder and is squeezing it as if to let him know that he's proud of him, and the judge is banging her gavel real hard and fast and shouting, "Order! Order in the court!" until it gets quiet.

"Your honor, this is ridiculous!" Aaron Mitchell says loudly. He's so angry his face is turning red. "If you recall, judge, I expressed to you in chambers my concern about the attendance of the children at the trial. I was afraid something like this might happen."

"Sit down, counselor! I am not certain yet what has happened. Young man!" She's talking to Jeremy and she doesn't look very happy. "Is this some kind of joke?"

"No, ma'am," Jeremy says firmly. "I wouldn't joke about my mom."

The judge's face softens. She is looking at him and he's looking back at her. After a minute she says, "Very well. I want to read what you say is your mother's journal. And it had better be everything you say it is. Do you understand me?"

"Yes, ma'am."

"I would certainly understand if you got upset by some of the things you've heard this morning, and I could excuse your outburst. I could not excuse your misleading this court or falsifying evidence. Do you understand what I mean by 'falsifying evidence'?"

"I think so. Would that be like in the O. J. Simpson trial when his lawyer said the police made up evidence?"

The judge smiles a little. "Yes. I guess you could say that."

"This is really my mom's diary. You'll see."

"Very well."

"Your honor!" It's Aaron Mitchell. "This is highly unusual. There is no way to authenticate this diary, and it has not been introduced as evidence."

"Keep your shirt on, Mr. Mitchell," the judge says. "This is an unusual case, a tragic one. And there are children involved. You opened the door, counselor, when you led your client to make certain claims about their mother, claims she is not here to verify or refute, claims which will be all over the news tonight. We're dealing here with the reputation of a well-known artist and the mother of these children. This diary may be her only chance to be heard."

Aaron Mitchell is still upset. "If you admit this—this unverified document into evidence, I will file an appeal."

"I would expect nothing less, counselor. Court will reconvene at two o'clock."

I've been looking at Dad, who's still sitting on the witness stand. After glaring at Jeremy when he first stood up, Dad's head dropped. He looks like a balloon that has had all the air taken out as he gets up, and a guard comes and takes him out a side door, his lawyer and Grandfather Eric following.

"Where'd you find that?" I ask Jeremy.

"In the back of the bottom drawer of the file where Mom kept all her drawings."

"Why didn't you tell me, you creep?"

"I didn't tell anybody. I was afraid somebody would take it from me."

"What did Mom say?"

A man in a uniform comes over and asks Jeremy for the diary. Jeremy gives it to him. "It's my mom's," he says solemnly.

He smiles. "I'll tell the judge to take good care of it."

"Thanks."

As soon as the guard starts to move away, reporters rush up to where we're sitting and start shouting at Jeremy.

"What's in the diary?"

"Where did you find it?"

"How old are you?"

"Do you want to your father to go to prison?"

Gloria Miller hurries over and pushes herself between us and the reporters. "The family doesn't want to talk to the press. Sorry, guys."

Gloria signals for one of the guards, who comes over and starts gently moving the reporters out of the courtroom. Jeremy is still standing. He looks like he's in a trance.

Jeremy

Grampy is hugging me real hard.

"I'm so proud of you, Jeremy. That took a lot of courage."

Then Gran and Karen and Jen all give me a hug and tell me how proud they are of me. I didn't really do anything, though, and I don't feel courageous. I didn't even know I was going to do that. It was just that I got so mad listening to what Dad was saying. I don't think I've ever been so mad in my life. I wasn't courageous. I just couldn't let Dad get away with lying like that.

Gloria says she is going to have sandwiches brought in for us and asks us what we want. After we give her our orders, Jenna puts her arm around my shoulder and we go sit where the jury was sitting.

"How're you doing?" she wants to know.

"I'm doing okay. How're you doing?"

"Okay, I guess. When you were standing there talking to the judge, you had this angry look on your face and you looked just like Mom."

"No way!"

"You did. I swear you did! God, it reminded me of all the times Mom got angry at me. What did Mom say about me in her diary? Was there stuff about me in there?"

"There was a lot about you. She didn't like it that you and Dad were together so much. Did Dad do something to you? Mom wrote how she was afraid that Dad was, well, you know."

Jenna looks sad. "Yeah. I know. I guess that's what I wanted her to think. But I hoped she knew me better. Everything got so fucked up! And it's probably all my fault."

"What're you talking about?"

"Nothing. It's okay. Just something I probably should've done and didn't because I'm a self-centered little bitch. What else did Mom say?"

"I don't know. A lot of it I didn't understand but at the end she wrote something about Dad and some girl. That's how come I know Dad's lying."

"It's all my fault! It's all my fault!" Jenna exclaims and starts crying. Karen hurries over, and Jenna throws herself into Karen's arms. She's crying like she did that day in Miss Worthing's office.

"What's wrong, Jenna? What is it?" Karen asks.

Jenna doesn't say anything but keeps on crying. Karen takes her to the back of the courtroom, and I go sit with my grandparents.

"What if the judge doesn't believe what Mom wrote in her diary?" I ask Grampy.

"I think she'll believe it," Grampy responds.

"Why didn't you tell us you'd found her diary?" Gran asks. "What if you'd lost it?"

"But I didn't," I tell her.

"No, but you should have told us. Or some adult."

"I didn't want anyone to take it away from me. It's my mom's."

A delivery man comes in through the side door with our sandwiches. Karen and Jenna come up to the front and we all eat in silence.

After we finish, one of the guards comes with a plastic trash bag and we put all our garbage in it. He says we aren't supposed to eat in the courtroom and that Gloria got permission from the judge so we could. We make a special effort not to leave anything behind, not even a crumb.

I go over to Jenna. "Are you all right?"

"I don't know," she says. "I don't know."

Just then one of the guards comes in and tells us that the judge will be coming back in fifteen minutes. A few minutes later, Dad, Grandfather Eric, and Dad's lawyer come in. The lawyer and Dad sit down at the table. Grandfather Eric goes and sits in the first row right behind Dad and his lawyer. Finally, Judge Livingstone comes back and sits down in her big chair.

"Is the court reporter present?"

"Here, your honor," says the man who writes down everything everybody says.

"This is not a formal court session but a conference that would have been held in my chambers except for the number of people who should be present. Bailiff, are the doors locked? We don't want some enterprising reporter coming in."

"The doors are locked, judge," the man in the uniform says.

"Very well. I have read Rachel Pierce's diary and what she wrote tells a very different story than what we heard on the stand this morning from the defendant. According to her, she did not meet the defendant at an exhibition. She was one of his clients, and during that time their relationship became sexual. Further, she was afraid the defendant was involved in a similar kind of relationship with their daughter, though she refused to believe it. Finally, and most damning, is the entry she wrote on the last night of her life. It appears that she found letters written to the defendant by a student at the college that discussed, and it seems in graphic detail, a sexual relationship this young woman was having with the defendant, who may have been her therapist also. Rachel Pierce went on to write that she had made appointments for the next day, the day of her murder, with an attorney and with the president of Birchfield College. She was seeing the attorney to start divorce proceedings and she was going to see the president to give him one of the student's letters to her husband discussing their affair. I called the attorney and verified that Rachel Pierce did have an appointment for eleven on the morning of her death, and the attorney confirmed that the purpose was to discuss getting a restraining order and to start divorce proceedings. I also spoke with Ralph Hillman, the president of Birchfield College, and he confirmed that Rachel Pierce had called him the day before her death to make an appointment. When I asked him if he knew why Ms. Pierce wanted to meet with him, he said she claimed to have proof that her husband was having an affair with a student."

"Your honor!"

It's Dad!

"May I address the court?"

"Please."

"My wife was a very sick woman. I did not realize how sick until now. What you and my son see as proof are graphic examples of the kinds of delusions she was afflicted with. Anyone who dared think I would jeopardize my position by having an affair with a student who was also a client is obviously fantasizing."

Jenna starts crying.

Dad's lawyer jumps up. "Your honor! I must again renew my request that the children not be allowed to witness these proceedings. This is obviously an emotionally difficult time for them. In the interests of the children, could you ask the grandparents to take them home?"

"Just shut up!" Jenna yells, jumping to her feet. "Just shut the fuck up! What th' hell do you know about us? You're pissed because we wouldn't get on the stand and lie about Mom like you wanted us to."

"I beg your pardon!" the judge says, looking from Jenna to Dad's lawyer. "Is what she said true?"

Jenna doesn't hear the judge, because she keeps on talking. "Dad? How can you sit there and say that about Mom? Please don't do this!" The tears are really coming down her face. "Please!"

Dad looks at her like he doesn't know what she's talking about. "I am telling the truth, sweetheart. I'm sorry, but you didn't know your mother like I did."

"And she didn't know you like I did, and I'm so sorry I didn't tell her." Jenna is sobbing and talking, and it's kind of hard to understand what she's saying until she wipes her eyes and Karen gives her a tissue and she blows her nose. "Your honor, last June I was in town with some friends and when it was time to go home I went by my dad's office to get a ride home with him. I did that sometimes. This is his office in town."

"Jenna! Be quiet!" Dad says suddenly.

Jenna acts like she doesn't hear him. "There're two parts to his office—an outer part where you wait and then another room down a short hall where he meets clients. When I went in I was surprised that the outer office was dark. I thought maybe Dad had left and forgotten to lock the door. I tried the door to the inner office and it was unlocked so I started down the hallway toward Dad's office. Then I heard these sounds. And then I heard Dad's voice and then I heard a woman's voice. They—they weren't talking. I knew what they were doing. Then I heard him call her name. I haven't seen my mom's diary, but would it be proof, your honor, if the name I heard is the same one as in Mom's diary?"

"It would sure be more than coincidence."

"Dad said, 'Oh, Diane. Oh, Diane. It's so good.'"

The judge opens Mom's diary and turns until she finds the page and she reads: "'Her name is Diane and she is a junior at the college. . . . I wonder if Diane was one of Eric's clients, and how many other Dianes and Rachels have there been in the past fifteen years?'"

Jen looks at Dad. "For God's sake, Dad. Please stop lying. Jeremy and I need you to tell the truth!"

Dad looks over at me and Jen. I think I see tears in his eyes.

He sighs, looks away, and then back at us. "I didn't mean to kill her. You have to believe me. I didn't mean to kill her." His voice is soft.

"That's enough, Eric. Don't say anything more," his lawyer says.

Dad shakes his head. "I'm tired. I can't do this anymore."

"What happened that morning, Dr. Richards?" the judge asks.

"Your honor, I want the record to show that anything my client says is against the advice of counsel," the lawyer says.

"So noted, counselor. You may go on, Dr. Richards, if you wish."

"I do, your honor."

Even though he's supposed to be talking to the judge, he is turned toward us, as if Jenna and I are the real judges.

"I loved your mother, but she never really loved me. I loved her intelligence and how talented she was and how passionate she was about things. Something happened when we got married. One day she told me that she liked me better when I was her therapist. I realized then that she hadn't been attracted to me, Eric Richards. She had been attracted to Eric Richards, psychologist. I felt like a fool.

"But I thought that, in time, things would change, especially if we had children. But they didn't. So I—I—I started having affairs with—with students. Then, Diane."

He stops and licks his lips like he's nervous or scared. His lawyer pours him a glass of water from a pitcher on the table. Dad takes a sip.

"You came by the office that day," he continues, looking at Jenna. "You were sitting in the outer office when Diane and I came out. I was surprised to see you there, and Diane panicked. When I asked you how long you'd been sitting there, you said you'd just come in, but you said it in a way that I knew you were lying. It was almost as if you wanted me to know you were lying.

"That's when things started to get out of control. I was afraid you would tell Rachel about Diane. But you didn't. Instead, you started lying around in bikinis like you wanted to seduce me and asking me to put suntan lotion on you. And you were very beautiful and I found myself enjoying touching you, found myself thinking things I didn't want to think. You knew. Didn't you?"

Jenna nods. "I was flattered and grossed out at the same time."

Dad nods. "Then there was Diane. She started writing me those letters Rachel saw. I tried to stop seeing her, but the same day Rachel wrote in her diary that she was going to see the college president, Diane said she was going to report me to the president if I didn't leave Rachel. The next morning, when Rachel told me she was going to see President Hillman that day, it was the last straw. The only way out was to convince Rachel not to tell Hillman. I wouldn't contest the divorce. That would keep Diane quiet. I went to town to beg her not to tell Hillman."

"Why did you take the gun? And where did you get it?" the judge wants to know.

"I took the gun just to scare her. That's all I was intending to do. I've had a gun ever since I had a practice in New York. While I was in training, a client threatened to kill me. It's licensed. I keep it at my office in town."

"Go on, Dr. Richards."

"When I saw Rachel coming out of Sutter's, I asked her if we could go somewhere and talk. She refused. She said she had one of Diane's letters and she was going to ruin me, that she wanted a divorce, that she was going to take you and Jeremy with her and I would not be allowed to see either of you, and that she was going to fix it so I wouldn't be able to practice psychology anywhere in America. She wanted to know how many others there had been, and I lied and told her Diane was the only one since I'd married her. She didn't believe me. I didn't care. I had to have that letter back. That's when I pulled the gun out. The next thing I knew she was lying on the pavement. I saw something sticking out the back pocket of her jeans and I pulled on it. It was the letter from Diane. I took it, went home, and ran the letters through the shredder and then went and sat on the front step and waited for the police. I knew my life was over, and I'm sorry now that I didn't have the guts to kill myself. I just hope you and Jeremy can forgive me someday."

Jenna doesn't say anything. Neither do I. The judge asks the lawyers to come forward, and they are talking together. I can't hear what they're saying. Dad is looking at me and Jenna like he wants one of us to give him a hug or something.

I want to go. I'm tired.

Jenna

THE CEMETERY

It's over. The judge sentenced Dad today. He got life in prison without the possibility of parole, not only because he killed Mom but because he lied so much and tried to blame it on her. Grampy and Gran and Grandfather Eric were in court to hear the judge's decision, but Jeremy and I went to school.

So now it's like he's dead, too. Maybe I'll go see him sometime after I'm grown. Maybe after I get married and have kids I'll send him pictures or something. But maybe not. I mean, what am I supposed to tell my kids about why they don't have grandparents? I think I'll just tell them that they're dead and maybe after they're grown I'll tell them the truth. I mean, I might not even tell my husband, whoever he'll be.

Gregory called. Dad's trial was on TV in Albany and all about how Jeremy and I were the ones who made him confess. Gregory said he's staying with a friend and will be going to Chicago in a couple of weeks to live with his uncle. I asked him if he had stopped drinking, and he said he had but I'm not sure. He told me he was sorry things turned out how they did between us, that he really liked me and all, but he couldn't hold it together the way I seemed to. I told him about the web page. It's up and I don't know how, but kids are finding it! Bob gave me a brand-new computer! Gave it to me! Every day when I get home from school, I log on to the web page and there's always somebody new who's written something about his or her parent who died. Some of the stories are really sad, worse even than when Dad killed Mom. Today a kid wrote in from Kosovo and talked about how soldiers killed his mom and dad. His English wasn't that great, but what he was saying was still pretty hard to take. I wonder why dads kill moms but moms don't kill dads. Or maybe moms do it, too. Just in a different way.

It is warm. The last time I was here was the day of the funeral. The sun was shining then, too. I've thought a lot about coming but I was afraid. I don't know why. I just was. Now that Dad's been sentenced and I know what's going to happen to him, it's like I can breathe. I feel like I've been holding my breath ever since it happened. Holding my breath and feeling guilty for not telling Mom about Dad and Diane, feeling like she would be alive now if I had told.

The judge gave Mom's journal back to Jeremy and I started reading it, but I couldn't finish it and gave it back to him. I didn't know she was in so much pain. I didn't know how hard I was making things for her. Karen read it and told me I couldn't have known, that I'm only a kid. But I still feel like I should have told her about Dad and Diane. Gran said Dad would have just killed her sooner.

I walk slowly up the hill. There's a headstone on Mom's grave. I guess Gran and Grampy had it put there. All it has on it are her name and when she was born and when she died. I cut some forsythia from the bush in our yard on my way over here, and I lay them at the base of the headstone.

"Hi, Mom. It's over. I'm sorry I haven't been to see you, but I just couldn't come until now. I'm doing okay. I got straight As every quarter in school. Can you believe it? And I'm learning all about computers and doing some stuff with computer graphics. I wish you could see it. But what's so weird is that if you were still alive, I probably wouldn't have gotten straight As or be doing anything with computers. I'm sorry. I'm really sorry I wasn't a better daughter, but it's not too late. I'm going to be the best daughter I can and make you proud of me. I love you, Mom."

I didn't know I was going to say any of that, and I'm surprised at what came out. But it's true. Just because she's dead it doesn't mean I stopped loving her or that she stopped loving me. It's just her body that left. The love didn't.

I reach in the pockets of my jeans and take out the rings I had in my navel and nipple. They've been sitting on the top of my dresser since I took them out right before I went to the funeral home that night. I dig a little hole in the dirt on Mom's grave and drop them in. Then I cover it up and pat it down so nobody will notice anything.

Jeremy

THE HOUSE

The day after Dad's trial, I told Miss Albright I was going back to my room. Then I walked Sara to her room like I do every morning. She was worried about what was going to happen after school, since I wouldn't be in Miss Albright's room where she always came and got me. I told her I would wait at the door of the school for her.

It's okay being back in my own room. But it's not like it was before. I'm different now. Everything that happened at the trial, what I did and all, was in the papers and on television and the other kids seem like they look up to me now, like I know things they don't. And I do.

I told Mom I had to go to my house today, so I wouldn't be on the school bus and she should be home to meet Sara. She said she knew about the meeting with Mom's lawyer. I wonder how she knew.

It feels funny to call Elaine "Mom," but the other night at supper we had pork chops and they were so good and without thinking I said, "Mom, could I have another one?" Everything kind of stopped and it took me a second to realize what I had said. I started to apologize, but she said it was all right. I haven't done it anymore. At least not out loud. It's easier to call Bob "Dad," which I do all the time now.

I go in the studio and look around. I've moved most of my stuff over to Sara's house and practically all that's left is Mom's. I hear a car pull into the driveway and go to the door to see who it is. It's Miss Albright.

I go outside but don't bother to lock the door behind me. "Hi."

"Hi, Jeremy. How're you doing?"

"I'm okay."

She gets out of the car and I take her hand. "Thanks."

"For what?" she wants to know.

"Just thanks," I repeat.

"You're welcome."

Grampy and Gran pull in the driveway in their rental car, and behind them, Karen and Jenna. Grandfather Eric's already in the house.

"Well, where shall we sit?" Gran wants to know once everybody's out of the cars. "In the family room in front of the fireplace?"

"What about out on the deck?" Jenna suggests. I know she doesn't like to be inside the house.

So we sit around the picnic table, our grandparents on one side, me, Jenna, Karen and Miss Albright on the other. It's a little crowded, but I'm little for my age so it's all right. The only person who's not here yet is Mom's lawyer. Karen's cell phone rings, and when she gets off she says that was Mom's lawyer and she's going to be a half hour or so late.

"That'll give me enough time to say a few things." It's Grandfather Eric. His voice is sad and his body is hunched over. "I know you folks have some decisions to make, and I need to get on back to Pennsylvania. But there're some things I need to say."

He stops and rubs at his eyes, but more like he's tired than like he's about to cry. Then he looks at me and Jenna. "I don't want you to think that your father is an evil man. I'm not saying he didn't do evil things. Killing your mother was an evil thing. Having improper relationships with his clients was an evil thing. But I guess because I know something about why he did all the things he did, it's hard for me to say that he's an evil man. Maybe that's because I think I had something to do with it."

"What're are you talking about, Eric?" Grampy asks. "Surely you aren't saying you're to blame for what he did to Rachel?"

"No. I'm not saying that. But I'm not saying my hands are clean, either." He looks back at me and Jenna like there's something important he wants us to understand. "This business of being a person is complicated and confusing sometimes. I expect you two know something about that after all you've been through. Who you are and what you are is partly because of who your parents, your grandparents, and even the ones before them were, the ones whose names we don't even remember. We humans like to think we are free to choose our lives. Maybe we are. Maybe we aren't. I'm just not sure anymore.

"It wasn't until I heard what Eric said in court that I finally understood. I'm still not sure Eric does, or if he ever will. You would've thought that with both of us being in psychology that we would have talked about her. But we never did. It hurt too much. It still does."

Grandfather Eric wipes his eyes and this time there are tears.

"Jennifer was two years younger than Eric. I can't say who adored her more, me or him. She loved to draw, and when she came into a room, it was like the sun coming out from behind a cloud. No matter how good you were feeling, you always felt better when Jennifer was around.

"She was eight and Eric was ten when it happened. We were living in Philadelphia then. Our house was surrounded by a wrought-iron fence; our yard was filled with trees. Eric had climbed up into one of the trees, and Jennifer wanted to do everything Eric did. She climbed up after him. He says he told her not to. She kept climbing. He said that she had almost made it up to where he was and reached out her hand for him to take it and she lost her balance. That fence had points on it like spears and she fell onto one of them."

"Oh, my God, no!" Gran exclaims, putting her hand over her mouth. Everybody else gasps. Everybody except me. I think Grandfather Eric is trying to get us to feel sorry for Dad. I'm not going to.

"Eric blamed himself, and I did, too. I cut him out of my life. Dorothy told me I'd live to regret it. I didn't care. He thought he could make it up to me by becoming a psychiatrist like me." He looks at Karen. "That's why I wouldn't give him the money for graduate school and medical school. I didn't want anything to do with him."

"I'd always wondered if something had happened to Eric when he was young. So it was Jennifer he was trying to bring back when he named both his daughters Jenna."

It's Karen. What is she talking about?

Grandfather Eric nods his head.

"Dad had another daughter named Jenna?" I ask.

"My daughter," Karen says simply.

Dad and Karen had a daughter named Jenna? Wow!

Grandfather Eric continues. "I'm sorry he did what he did and then didn't own up to it. Rachel was a lovely girl," he says, looking at Grampy and Gran. "Talented, very bright, and I was always very fond of her. She was especially nice to me when Dorothy died. I'm sorry I've acted the way I have. I thought by getting involved in his defense the way I did that I could make up to him all the ways I'd neglected him. I was wrong for neglecting him and wrong for trying to make it up the way I did."

He looks at me. "I'm sorry for treating you like you were some enemy. You had more sense than I did and you knew your father better than I did. I'm sorry, Jeremy. Jenna, I owe you an apology, too, for trying to pressure you into testifying to make something seem like something it wasn't. I hope the two of you can forgive me and maybe even come see me sometime. If it wouldn't be too painful for you." He turns back to Grampy and Gran. "I'm sorry for what my son did to your daughter and our grandchildren."

He stands up. Grampy gets up and gives him a hug. When he's done, Gran gives him a hug, too. Then he and Karen hug. Jenna looks at me and I look back at her. I know what she's thinking and if she wants to hug him, she can. I'm not. But Jenna doesn't move. Grandfather Eric looks at us like he would hug us if we'd let him, but I pretend like I'm looking at something out in the field. Only when I hear his footsteps do I turn my head and watch him walk across the yard, get in his car, and drive away.

We sit there. Nobody knows what to say. Finally Gran asks, "Would anyone like something cold to drink?"

Everybody answers all at once, like we've just been released from an evil spell, and Karen and Miss Albright go with Gran to help her get the drinks. Just as they're bringing out a tray of sodas, Mom's lawyer arrives and sits down where Grandfather Eric was sitting.

The lawyer chitchats with everybody. I just wish they'd shut up and get on with it. Underneath the table Jenna reaches for my hand, and when I feel it, I reach back and we hold each other's hands real tight.

Finally, the lawyer says, "Well, we're here because there are some big decisions that need to be made. First and foremost is you two," she says to me and Jenna. "We have to look at the options of where you can live, whom you can live with, and the legal ramifications."

"What does legal ramifi—whatever mean?" I want to know.

"The law needs to know who is going to be legally responsible for taking care of you, for seeing that you have a place to live and food to eat, clothes to wear, and that you go to school every day."

"Sara's parents said I could live with them," I say immediately. "I've been living there anyway."

Mom's lawyer nods. "Yes. I know. They came to see me and inquired about what would be involved in adopting you. It seems that when Bob was a boy his parents adopted someone whose parents had died."

"So can he adopt me?" I want to know. I'm so excited I can hardly sit still.

"I think the court would approve if your grandparents do."

I look at them and am surprised to see them smiling.

"We had a long meeting with Bob and Elaine a few days ago," Gran begins. "I suppose I was hoping the two of you would come stay with us in San Francisco, but your grandfather and I had to face facts. We're not young anymore and the two of you need to be with people whose ways are younger. Will you come visit us?"

"We will," I say.

Nobody's said anything about what's going to happen to Jenna. She's squeezing my hand so hard it hurts, and I want to wiggle my fingers a little but I don't want her to think that she should let go. But just then Karen reaches over and touches Jenna's arm and Jenna lets go of my hand.

"Would—would you be my daughter?" Karen asks.

"You mean it?"

"Rachel and I used to talk about if anything happened to her and your father—like if they died in a car accident, airplane crash, or something—that she wanted me to adopt you and Jeremy. You and I have always been close."

"Can I change my name?"

Karen looks at her like she doesn't understand. I sure don't. "What do you mean?"

"I want my own name. I don't want a dead girl's name. And I don't want Dad's name. Mom wanted to name me Melissa. Can I be Melissa Pierce?"

Jenna is crying softly, and Karen puts her arms around her.

After a minute, Mom's lawyer says, "Well, maybe we should clear up these other matters at another time."

Wiping her eyes, Jenna turns to the lawyer. "No. That's all right. I'm okay. I just want to get it over with, whatever it is."

"Very well. This house."

Jenna and I look at each other and at the same time we say, "Sell it!"

The lawyer says that would have been her advice. She says some other stuff I don't understand about a financial adviser and investments. Then she wants to know what I want to do with Mom's paintings and drawings.

I've been thinking about that and have decided that my grand-parents, me, Jenna, Karen, and Miss Albright should each take one or two and then give the rest to the college. Mom's lawyer chuckles and says I can *sell* them to the college. Awesome!

"Then I guess we're done," the lawyer says.

Jen and I turn and look at each other. She looks really happy. I am, too. I don't feel like a homeless person anymore. But it's never going to be like it was. I'm going to be a big brother all the time now and a little brother only some of the time. But maybe Jenna will come over to my house sometime for dinner and to work on the web page with Dad, and then I can be little brother and big brother all at once.

"Are you really going to change your name?" I ask.

She nods. "It's creepy being named for two dead girls. It's like I was never me to him. There's been this ghost living in our fam-ily and we didn't even know it."

"Maybe it was the ghost that killed Mom."

Miss Albright looks like she's getting ready to leave, and I go over to where she's talking to my grandparents, who are thanking her. I take her hand and we go to the studio.

"So. Which one of Mom's paintings do you want?"

She shakes her head. "Jeremy, that's very generous but you don't have to do this."

"I know. I want to. Look around. I have to go do something. I'll be back in a little while."

I go downstairs and pick up my backpack, the one Mom made me. Then I go in the garage and find a garden spade and put it in the pack. As I start across the field, Jen calls to me. "Hey, Jeremy! Where're you going?"

"I'll be back in a few minutes" is all I say.

"You want to go for pizza later with everybody?"

"Sure."

"Don't be long."

"I won't."

This is the first time I've been here since after Christmas. The the headstone looks nice. A few branches of forsythia lie in front of the headstone. I wonder who put them there.

I kneel beside the grave, open my backpack, and take out the diary. I wrapped it in plastic and sealed it up with heavy tape. The earth is soft and not much grass is growing on her grave yet. I take out the spade and quickly scoop out a deep hole, put the diary in it, cover it up, and pat the earth down until you can't tell anybody's been digging here.

I sit for a few minutes, kind of like I used to when Mom would be cooking. I never had anything to say then and I don't now, either. I'm glad, though, that I won't have to go away and leave Mom all alone.

I hear a bird. I look up but can't find it. Then, off in the distance, I hear the same birdcall. Then the bird near me answers, and a few seconds later the bird in the distance calls back.

Smiling, I get up, brush off my pants, and walk slowly away.

Author's Note

I am often asked where I get my ideas. Books, and especially fiction, do not proceed from ideas. They are born from feelings, and more, from wondering. I see someone walking along the street and wonder: Who is he? Where is he going? Where does he live? I look at a clerk in a store and wonder if she is going to be happy to go home when she gets off work or is there some sorrow and pain awaiting her there. When I read the newspaper or watch the news on television, I wonder what it was like for the people who died in an airplane crash, and what it was like for their families when they learned of the death of the son or daughter they just put on the plane or were going to the airport to meet. Perhaps one of the writer's tasks is to weave himself into others' pain.

A painful and sad truth of our time is that fathers kill mothers, and when I see on television or read in the newspaper about another such murder, I wonder: What is it like for the children? What do you do, what do you feel, where do you go, how do you cope when your father kills your mother?

Writing takes place in the mind before one sits down to the computer (in my case). I write entire pages in my head while at the same time searching for the book's overall structure. After months of this (and sometimes years) there comes a magical moment when the book is suddenly alive inside me, when I have a sense of what the book is about and where it might be going, and

I am overwhelmed by the feeling that if I do not begin typing, I will die.

So it was with *When Dad Killed Mom*. I am Jewish and do not work on the Sabbath, and that includes turning on the computer. But there came a Saturday afternoon when everything—characters, voice, place, story line—came together and I had to sit down and begin typing because such moments come only once. (I think every writer is haunted by the story of the English poet, Samuel Taylor Coleridge, interrupting the writing of "Kubla Khan" to answer the door and never being able to finish it.) Almost as if I were in a state of possession, I wrote twenty pages in one sitting, something I had never done in my more than thirty years as a published author. But the voices and personalities of Jeremy and Jenna were fully realized from the moment I began typing. I knew them intimately and they knew me.

Usually I am dispassionate when I write—in other words, I do not experience emotionally what I am writing—and so I seldom laugh, even if I know that what I've written is funny, and I never cry. At least not until *When Dad Killed Mom*. I cried while writing the first draft; I cried during subsequent revisions; I cried when going over the galleys. But Charles Dickens cried when he wrote his books, so I figured it was all right if I cried for "my" characters.

However, it was obvious to me that in writing about Jenna and Jeremy, I was also writing from a sense of personal grief. Since childhood I have endured the deaths of many people, and though I've never known anyone whose father killed his or her mother, I grew up with children who suffered the death of a parent. Among my students at the University of Massachusetts there have been many who have buried a parent and others who had a parent die during the school year. And I wondered: How did they, being so young, find the way to endure and persevere? So, as I wrote and cried, I was grieving for them all—and for myself.

When Dad Killed Mom is fiction, but the emotions it explores are not. Fathers killing mothers is so much a part of the norm that we scarcely notice anymore. The most invisible victims are the children. Maybe through reading about Jeremy and Jenna, we will allow ourselves to wonder about the actual children.

Julius Lester
Belchertown, Mass.
21 November 2000